THE STOLEN COAST

THE STOLEN COAST

COAST

DWYER MURPHY

VIKING

VIKING
An imprint of Penguin Random House LLC
penguinrandomhouse.com

LIBRARY OF CONGRESS CATALOGING–IN–PUBLICATION DATA

Names: Murphy, Dwyer, author.
Title: The stolen coast / Dwyer Murphy.
Description: [New York] : Viking, [2023]
Identifiers: LCCN 2022053762 (print) | LCCN 2022053763 (ebook) |
ISBN 9780593653678 (hardcover) | ISBN 9780593653685 (ebook)
Subjects: LCGFT: Thrillers (Fiction) | Novels.
Classification: LCC PS3613.U7284 S76 2023 (print) |
LCC PS3613.U7284 (ebook) | DDC 813/.6—dc23/eng/20221122
LC record available at https://lccn.loc.gov/2022053762
LC ebook record available at https://lccn.loc.gov/2022053763

Printed in the United States of America
1st Printing

DESIGNED BY MEIGHAN CAVANAUGH

For Carolina and Eloisa

PART I

1

Tommy Carvalho was featherweight champion in the Police Athletic League when he was fifteen years old. That might not sound like much of a title to you or me, but for Tommy it was a point of pride. He married young, straight out of high school, and developed an addiction to Vicodin that he managed to kick, possibly by reminding himself that for a span of time in his golden youth there wasn't another boy on the South Coast of Massachusetts who could knock him down. The marriage ended after a year. He still saw his ex-wife regularly and liked to cook her dinner once or twice a week, without asking questions about how she spent the rest of her time or affections. We had never been very close growing up, but Tommy was part of my Thursday evening pickup basketball game. Most of the year we played at the Y, but in summer we went to the beach. It was five a side, full court, and Tommy was an able if slightly undersized wing who liked to run. He had a carelessness about him on the court that I always admired. Whenever I pulled a rebound, I looked for him streaking down the sidelines.

In the time since he cleaned up, Tommy had taken over as the head of Parks and Recreation. He was the one who had suggested laying the new blacktop on the public beach courts several years before, and whenever we wanted to play late, he carried a master key to turn on the lights. We would all throw in a dollar or two afterward, toward the electricity bill. It seemed to me he had settled into a nice, tranquil life, all things considered, and it surprised me that summer when he brought up the possibility of escape. At first, I took it for a joke, but after he kept finding ways of steering the conversation back in that direction, I decided there was probably more to it.

"You should take a vacation," I suggested. "Go somewhere warm. Have a cocktail."

"I don't want a vacation," he said. "We've got beaches right here."

"Then go somewhere cold. Fly to Iceland. It's light out all night."

"I'm not some goddamn tourist," he said.

That was the problem. When you got right down to it, Tommy had a lot of pride.

"Well," I said. "Tell me where you want to go."

"Somewhere they won't find me."

"Who's they?"

The question only made him upset. In addition to the pride, Tommy had a temper. We were sitting at a table outside Alphonse's café, across the street from the playground. The court lights were still on, and they cast a strange, sidelong glow over Tommy's gaunt features.

"Look," I said. "Unless you've got a reason, there's no point in dwelling on it. It's not something you do for recreation. You've got to have a plan and a hell of a motivation."

"I've got one," he said. "You wouldn't understand, but I've got a motivation all right."

"What is it?"

He leaned in close and lowered his voice. Before, he'd been bellowing.

"Ever wake up in the morning and you don't recognize yourself?"

"Sure. Everyone does."

"Maybe, I don't know about everyone. I know what I see: a fucking stranger."

"You think you won't see a stranger if you wake up in France?"

"Who said anything about France, for Chrissake?"

It was true, nobody had. I pulled another beer out of the bucket, and we talked for a while about the game. Talking about pickup was never simple. Our weekly crew had twelve, but we usually brought out three or four irregulars. The losers would have to regroup and shoot for the right to play again, with an informal agreement that a man shouldn't be left out more than a game at a time. The teams therefore disassembled and re-formed with new pieces and styles, and it was difficult to speak of a single game in any meaningful way, unless there had been a winning streak. Instead, you had to talk about feel and flow and other vague notions that brushed up against the spiritual. That night Tommy and I had played together twice. We lost one and came back to win the other. It was early in the summer and the ball rolled off your fingers differently outside.

"I just want to know how it could be done," Tommy said later.

I was looking for a waiter to pay.

"I think I'd feel better if I knew," he said. "Like a mantra."

"I thought your stint was in Old Colony."

"It was. So what?"

"They don't have mantras in Old Colony. That's a stone-cold outfit."

"The hell they don't. You were never there, were you? That's one place I've been."

He stuck his hand into the ice melt at the bottom of the bucket where the beer had been.

Old Colony was the prison where he once served two months on a criminal responsibility evaluation.

His mood had darkened over the course of the night. It was mean of me to tease him.

"Look," I said, "if you really want to know, come by the office. We'll talk."

That perked him up and got his fist out of the water. "You mean that?" he asked.

"Sure, anytime. Come by tomorrow."

"I can't tomorrow."

"Sunday, then."

He shook his head. "Sunday, I'm cooking for Mila."

"For fuck's sake, Tommy, come when you can. Whenever you're motivated."

Before I had a chance to pay the check a fight broke out on the street beside the café. Somebody had said something to one of the waiters. Alphonse always kept a lot of tough waiters on staff. Most of them were his nephews, and they would come from around New England for a few months to make money with their uncle. His place stayed busy right up until closing at midnight. The waiter who was involved in the fight was a big kid of eighteen or nineteen who was holding on to some of his baby fat.

Tommy jumped into the middle of it. He was giving up five inches to one of the boys and forty pounds to the other, but Tommy was quick and moved well, even on the ground, where the fight was mostly happening. I wondered briefly if I had it wrong about him. Maybe he had wrestled or fought jujitsu. No, it was boxing. Featherweights. He had told me about it a few times.

The fight lasted ten or twenty seconds that seemed to stretch out much longer. Tommy got the boys separated, and one of them said something in Portuguese and the other wiped down his jeans, which were torn at the knee and had mud streaks up to the belt.

When he got back to the table, I asked Tommy if he felt better.

"Go to hell," he said. "They're just kids, for Chrissake. What are they angry about?"

"What were you?"

"Go to hell," he said again. "I got my reasons."

I put down an extra twenty on top of the bill for the kid who had been in the fight, the one who still had his baby fat, and walked home along the marina, counting the boats.

2

Onset is a small community in the southeastern corner of Massachusetts, next to Cape Cod. If the canal had been built a few miles to the west, the town's fate might have been different. Things as they were, it was a way station. On Cranberry Highway the water park drew a crowd in summer. There were gas stations that charged less than you would find across the bridge and motels that would take cash and let you check in without showing an ID. The harbor was shaped like a teardrop, with the public beach running half a mile around it. Along the waterfront were restaurants, cafés, and a few bars that served one or two modest dishes, usually something simple the bartenders had prepared themselves. Near the village center there were more motels, and in the river neighborhoods you could rent a two-room cottage by the month, week, or night.

It was a run-down place and fairly picturesque for those

who had a romantic streak. Over the years Onset had gained a reputation as a place you could go to live anonymously for a while, no matter who you were or what you had done. There were always towns like that in out-of-the-way places. The experience in Onset, however, was somewhat more deliberate. A lot of careful work went into it. Sometimes it seemed like just about everyone you saw there was on the run from something. In other moments, stasis hung over the town like a cloud of gas and you would see the same faces night after night, and it felt like low tide would go on forever and the wind would always die in the flats.

I was renting a small cottage on Shore Drive that year, across from the beach. It was only a five-minute drive from the house where I'd grown up, but it felt to me like progress. In the mornings I could go for a swim before breakfast, then walk to the office.

Work was busy during the summer, and it kept me often outdoors. My father, who had built the business and was largely responsible for the town's status as an organized haven, believed in the old tradecraft and had infected me with a certain fetish for it too. I made daily rounds on foot, clearing out the dead drops and checking on proverbial curtains and fence posts for the signals that meant one of our clients was looking to talk.

Logistics and transport was how the business was described in our tax filings. The corporate charter was out of Delaware and belonged to a holding company in the Grand Caymans. I had gone there once to look at the post office boxes. The bank accounts were in Panama by way of Miami. All the same, it was a profession that required a personal touch. That was one of the things I liked about it. Walking down High Street and around the harbor in the mornings, I always had people to say hello to.

I went by the office a few times that week to see if Tommy had come but there was no word from him. He didn't show up at the pickup run that Thursday either, and I wondered vaguely if he had finally decided to take that vacation. We played until eight, and when it started getting dark a few of the guys turned on the lights of their cars because Tommy wasn't there to open up the electricity box. That was when I decided to go.

Once you thought about leaving pickup you had to do it, or else in the next moments or the next game you would pull a hamstring or knock somebody to the blacktop and split their skull. Or nothing would happen but you would know you were on borrowed time. It was all superstition, playground mythology, but everyone believed in it, so I left.

"Find fucking Tommy," somebody called after me, and I said that I would.

Maybe they thought because I helped people disappear, I could find them too. Or else they were only annoyed about playing in the dark. Headlights never gave you enough.

I STILL HAD A FEW STOPS to make that night and took them in order, moving through the neighborhoods in erratic circles and occasionally pulling into driveways where nobody lived. In all those years I had never been followed in Onset. It was the ritual that was important, more than the caution. There was always a chance law enforcement might be around, but it was only a small chance. We had a long-standing arrangement with the local force. The nearest state trooper barracks was thirty miles away in Yarmouth. There was a federal task force in New Bedford. My cousin worked for it. Mostly they were focused on harassing fishermen and what was left of the old dock unions. In exchange for a monthly stipend, Camila, my cousin, fed us tips. The tips were hardly ever relevant to anything we were doing, but I knew that was the point: evidence of absence.

It occurred to me now and again that I would never perform the basic functions of the work so well as my father had. He had been properly trained, for starters. My apprenticeship was more haphazard. He always told me that the tradecraft was illusory, or even insignificant, like all sacred things. That was the way he liked to conduct a lesson: in the murky ground between sophistry and aphorism. It was the kind of job you had to learn by experience, he maintained, and by talking to people. Always talking, then letting them have a turn, and in the silences and patterns, you were meant to learn something that was true. More than the particulars of the job, it was the atmosphere. The technology around surveillance and espionage changed all the time. There would only ever be more cameras in the world. We leave traces of ourselves behind; nothing's erased. In my father's day, a person could well and truly vanish. That would soon be over, if it wasn't already.

Still, you tried following protocol. It was meant to help. You checked mirrors and looked out for watchers. You tightened the circles, then let the slack back into them.

I was alone; nobody following, nobody interested. The streets were dark and clear.

Driving into the village center, I made a note of vacant houses and their addresses. The town seemed so quiet on the outskirts, but as you got closer to the shore, you heard a hum off the water. It was sheltered coast and there was hardly any surf, but the water was never completely quiet; it was always moving, and it sounded like a body heaving.

When I was young my father told me stories about the town's past as a smuggler's cove. They turned out to be untrue. The truth was stranger, and I had never asked him whether he knew it and had decided not to tell me or if there was some other reason why he'd invented the pirates. The first Europeans to settle in Onset were wreckers. There was a clan or a tribe or a group of them living in a cluster of lean-tos about a hundred yards up one of the inlets off Buzzards Bay. They would lie in wait for shipwrecks and salvage what they could. They would move buoys in the boating channels and distort the beams from the Wickham lighthouse in order to confuse the ships and encourage them into the rocks. Captains were sometimes bribed or paid off. This carried on right until the turn of the century, when the governor cleared them out.

At one point, the town was used as a retreat for Boston Spiritualists. They believed the land had been sacred to the Wampanoag who fished there. Séances were held during the summer solstice and then again in September, when the breeze was good and it tended not to rain. A few of the Spiritualists built homes, sprawling manors situated with a mind toward communing with the dead, but mostly the old Boston families, even the very eccentric ones, set down seasonal roots on the other side of the tributaries: on Cape Cod.

Onset was for fishermen. Mainly Portuguese, Cape Verdean, and Azorean, though there were Pacific Islanders, too, and a good number of Sicilians. The Irish came from Boston and New York after World War II and tried to take over the docks and the police force but didn't have much luck with it. Onset was a free port at heart. The bars and cafés were always well run, and you could get a good, cheap meal so long as you ate fish or clams.

A lot of drugs passed through as well. I didn't move any myself. It was a matter of pragmatism, not principle. There was too much competition in drugs. Only a few people could get you across a border safely with a new name, professional credentials, and reliable residency status. Traffickers never interfered with our work. On the contrary, they mostly approached it with a deference that bordered on the absurd. They wanted to know that there was a way out for them too. Everybody wanted that.

For a long time, I subscribed to the wisdom that it was necessary work, and there was a profound, if fleeting, satisfaction to be found in its inevitability. That was the sort of thing your mind got onto while you were driving in circles. Lately, I had begun to wonder how much of the wisdom I had received naively. The truth is, I had hardly traveled anywhere myself. I had only crossed a lot of borders and driven into towns and cities, then turned back. It was a parochial life, even if it didn't always feel that way.

3

The tables outside Alphonse's were crowded and I didn't feel like seeing anyone, so I drove to Marianne's. Marianne was a petite Malaysian woman who had ridden the highs and lows of the tiki lounge business for years and would carry on serving drinks in a choice of hurricane or coconut glass long after the rest of us were gone. The main room was quiet and cool, and there were two screens above the bar, one for keno and one for the Red Sox, neither with any sound. Marianne was sitting at one end of the bar.

"Four innings," she said. "Four innings and they're already using up the bullpen."

Marianne had several Pedro Martínez jerseys hanging above the bar and judged the current pitching staff against that impossible standard. It was a down year for the Red Sox. She used to walk around the village late at night, after games, looking forlorn. That summer she had hired a DJ to play, starting at

10:30 p.m. Whether she had a permit to do it, and how she kept her neighbors on the bluffs from complaining, I didn't know. The DJ was a Brazilian kid from Hyannis who played reggaeton from a computer and would sometimes post flyers around town on telephone poles and in public bathrooms.

The Red Sox had no middle or long relief to speak of that year. The game was as good as lost. Marianne thought so too. To pass the time, she was telling a woman three stools down a story that hung together loosely but was related with a lot of verve. It had some interesting locales, starting in Marianne's hometown, Klang, part of the old maritime Silk Road, and somehow ending up in Casablanca, in Morocco, another port town. What she was really talking about was the Red Sox, though it took her some time to come back around to the subject.

"*Casablanca* built that team," she said, pointing at a pennant above the bar, commemorating the World Series win in 2004. "Bet you didn't know that, did you?"

It was a story I had heard her telling before, only I hadn't realized it until just then.

Casablanca, the movie, was written by Julius and Philip Epstein along with Howard Koch, who was later blacklisted. Philip was the grandfather of Theo Epstein, the Red Sox general manager, whom Marianne held in very high regard, almost as high as the regard she held for Pedro Martínez, though she didn't keep any of his portraits around the bar. Pedro had a very inviting smile. It was the kind you wanted to see in a convivial setting.

The story kept on going and listening to it was a strange kind of balm. I was watching the game, too, which carried on with or without our attention. The Sox kept falling further back, thanks to their bullpen. You got the feeling it would never reach the ninth.

I was getting ready to leave when a group from the Cape came in. There were six or seven of them, and you knew they were from the Cape, or on their way, from their clothes and their boat shoes and from the way they smiled very carefully on entering, like they were trying to prove their courage. One of them ordered drinks at the bar and called out to the others to find out what they wanted. They wanted light beers to a man, then a few more came in and the place was crowded. It happened quickly, the way a summer storm comes to shore.

That was when I saw Elena. The door swung open and she was between two boys wearing sweaters despite the heat. I wasn't sure she was with them, but then the kid at the bar kept calling out about the drinks and she told him she wanted rum, dark rum in a coconut shell. He looked bashful about ordering it that way but soon found the resolve.

She was wearing espadrilles and jeans and glasses that I didn't believe she needed, although they suited her fine, and she seemed to be in high spirits. Returning home following a long absence can have that effect, especially in summer when the air is heavy with salt and there are Cape boys ordering light beers and crowding around you.

I paid for my drink and went out the side door to the porch where the smokers were. Above the porch was a room with lace curtains and a soft light behind them. I had never noticed it before and wondered if it was Marianne's room or if she rented it out.

"You weren't going to leave like that, were you?"

Elena had come outside behind me. She was looking up at the bedroom light.

"I always knew they'd get you for voyeurism," she said. "Did you see the story about that motel in Colorado? The owner drilled peepholes into guests' walls. Kept it going for years—decades, maybe, nobody knows—through sheer force of yearning. I read it, thought of you. I wondered, What's old Jack up to these days? Sweet Jack. Kind Jack."

"The merchant marines," I said. "Got my card punched to sail."

"No, not that."

"French foreign legion."

She shook her head and hugged me and grazed a cheek against one of mine.

"Just passing through?"

"Always so serious," she said. "Professional Jack."

I thought about the last time I had seen her. It was in New York. Seven years before.

She was twenty-two then and heading off to law school under an assumed name.

"Are you parked nearby?" she asked. "Let's go for a drive, okay?"

"Won't they miss you inside?"

"They're nice boys. Don't look at them that way."

"What way?"

"You haven't joined the legion yet. Just take me for a goddamn drive."

She didn't want to go anywhere in particular, so I drove

out to Long Neck, where there were no stoplights or intersections but just a road that wound around the cemeteries and the cranberry bogs. At the end was a par 3 public course and a raggedy beach, and you could ease down the gears and make a loop around them and head back into town.

"It's been too long," she said. "I'm sorry I stayed away."

"That was the arrangement. Everyone needs an arrangement."

"Is that what it was?"

"A situation that calcified. It's the same thing."

"Strange, I thought we were lying low. Acting natural. Letting the world blow over."

She had one arm hanging outside. The other was getting in the way as I shifted gears. She said something about New York, how she had to get out. All those years gone, and that was how she explained herself, like it was a whim, like it was odd of me to wonder.

She was working me. It didn't matter. You were always getting worked. That's life.

"How long are you going to stay?" I asked.

"Maybe the summer. Or a few weeks. The plan's still calcifying."

"Is Mike joining you?"

"He's in London. A secret royalist, I think."

"Were those his cousins at the bar?"

"Why would they be?"

"He's old Cape, isn't he? Those families are always lousy with cousins."

"They're young, that's all. No reason to hate them."

"They never have to grow up. Isn't that a reason?"

"Let's just drive once around the harbor. I want to hear what the gulls are up to."

It sounded like she had a checklist of things she wanted to do, now that she was back in town: A beach visit at night. The seagulls over the harbor. A drive with one of her exes.

"Who was the girl?" she asked.

"What girl?"

"The one you were driving around with before me. I can smell her."

"Just a cousin of Mike's. One of the girl cousins."

"You don't need to hide things from me. It was a long time ago, wasn't it?"

"I've been spraying perfume on the seats all the while. Hoping you'd come back."

"Wouldn't that be nice though? You weren't one to suffer."

"That's the second time I've been told that tonight."

"From the other woman?"

"Pain and suffering. She wanted to talk about a case. A prospective client."

"God, what an interesting practice you must have. Nothing like New York."

I got the feeling she was going to tell me about something: the city or maybe work. She worked at a law firm now, and the last I'd checked, she was going to make partner. Elena had always inspired a lot of confidence in old men.

Instead, we kept driving in silence. I had taken us back to Cranberry Highway.

"Why don't we cross the bridge?" she said.

At that hour, the bridge had a lonesome feeling hanging over it. It was dark except for the spotlight on the Samaritan sign. Coming down, you could just make out the topiary they had carved into the center of the rotary, welcoming you to Cape Cod. The air always felt different on that side of the canal. Probably it had to do with the bay winds.

I didn't want to stay on the highway, so I turned back toward the canal.

"Could you pull over up there?" she said. "On the right. Just for a minute."

The road there had a narrow shoulder. I could only get two wheels onto the grass.

"I'll be right back," she said. "Turn off your lights, please."

Across the street, twenty yards down, was an old house that had been converted into a library annex and records building. I had been there once, while in school, to look at ships inside glass bottles. Or maybe it was the bottles themselves that were supposed to be interesting. It was never explained. The building was dark. It had been closed for hours.

She got out, crossed the road, and walked on the grass, which was covered in pine needles. The moon was out. Its light pierced through the pines and seemed to follow her steps. She approached the house slowly, without care, as though it were her own.

It was odd, watching her from that remove. It felt like a performance. A piece of theater. Like she knew that I was watching but was pretending not to in order to amplify something—the tension or the confusion. After working the lock for a minute, she let herself inside. Her movements seemed very deliberate, then for a stretch of time she was gone; disappeared. Like she had never come back. Seven years away and counting.

I turned the radio on and found some music.

Fifteen, twenty minutes passed. No lights turned on. She must have been carrying one.

When she came outside again, it was on the second floor. A widow's walk. She stood up there, leaning against a rail, looking calm, like a woman who had just awoken from a dream and was glad to find herself at home, with hours to sleep before morning.

My breath quickened, watching her. Both of my hands were on the wheel.

She came down by a trellis pinned to the building's side, covered in ivy that had spilled onto the shingling, looking natural about it. As far as I could tell, she wasn't carrying anything.

She got inside the Jeep and I turned onto the road, forgetting about the headlights for a moment until we reached a bend. The woods there, near the canal, were filled with deer. Neither of us was speaking. She wanted me to ask her, and I wasn't going to do it.

"It's incredible what they keep out in the open," she said. "All those records, blueprints, survey maps, assessments. You only have to know where to look and what you want."

"And the business hours. It's good to know whether they have alarms too."

"An alarm at a little records office like that? What for?"

The question hung between us for a moment.

"I'm planning something," she said. "It's still early, but it's coming together." In her tone, there was a note of suggestion. An enticement, or an invitation. "This is the best moment," she said. "Pure anticipation. Possibility."

"I don't need to hear about it, Elena."

"Are you sure?"

"Yes."

She looked out the window. In the darkness, the headlights caught the flash of eyes.

"I broke things off with Mike," she said. "Last week. A month ago, actually."

"I'm sorry."

"Don't be. He took it so well. It was after a party we gave. I told him it was over and he said why don't we do the dishes, in that case? He was drunk. I wasn't but for his sake I pretended to be. He washed and I dried and then put the dishes away. I broke one of them. Let it slip through my fingers and that seemed to satisfy him, like we'd really had it out. He swept it up into a little tray. Told me it was all right, he understood everything. Christ, six years was a long time for it to go on that way, don't you think?"

"I don't know. I've never been engaged."

"Any longer, we might have gone through with it. People do all kinds of things."

It sounded like she was going to tell me a few of them, then thought better of it.

We crossed under the Sagamore Bridge and kept going. Finally, she said we had better get back, we didn't want to hit traffic or get into any trouble with those deer. It was after midnight. There were no cars on the road. No boats in the canal, not even a barge.

The first lights we saw coming back into town were from a batting cage outside a go-kart track. The rest of the park was closed but the lights over the cages were on, and there was one old man inside hitting balls. He was batting lefty and had a clean swing.

"That'll be you one day," she said. "Do you still play basketball?"

"Once a week."

"That's good. I'm glad you do. I'll bet it's a comfort, having something like that."

"It's exercise."

"That's important too."

I was thinking about something else. A memory. The cottages we used to go inside in the off-season. Never taking anything but staying for a few hours or for a night and letting another life settle over us. I wondered whether she was thinking about it as well.

My phone buzzed. It was a message for a pickup and hold.

"I have to go," I told her.

She had looked away from the screen. She was discreet, in the end.

"Just pull over to the side," she said. "I'll hitchhike. What a lousy liar you are."

"It's work. I have to go to Stamford."

"Connecticut? Christ, at this hour. I take back what I said about your practice. Keep it."

"Why are you here, Elena? Can you tell me that? It's a simple question."

"I want to have some fun this summer. Do you remember what fun we had, Jack?"

I didn't say anything.

"I'm lying," she said. "I've been hired to abduct you. You're wanted in Geneva."

"Not Geneva. Zurich."

"Zurich, my mistake. The oligarchs want to discuss a matter with you. Very sensitive."

"I can't go. I don't want to miss the festival."

"The festival, that's right. I forgot about it. That's why I'm back. I came for the festival. Forget what I said about Switzerland. I was only testing you. Forget about it." She smiled and kept looking away. "Let's just drive back. You'll drop me off, won't you?"

I left her outside Marianne's. The reggaeton was still going. Her escorts were on the porch, smoking and talking. It was the start of summer, another season.

All the way to Stamford I kept playing back pieces of our conversation and remembering them slightly differently. It was like a recording that had been corrupted.

4

The Stamford client was a priority—a flash case, it was called. I was glad for the money, but it meant a lot of precautions I might not have had to take otherwise—moving people out of cottages, then going dark for a number of days and cleaning out secondary drops. There was a protocol to follow: a checklist dedicated to flash cases. The client was twenty-three years old. I picked him up in the taxi queue outside the Stamford Amtrak station. We were back in Onset by seven. He slept most of the drive.

There was an unsettled feeling in town that week and I knew that it would cause problems. Summer is never an easy season, no matter how much you want to enjoy it.

On Friday I got a complaint out of Pine Beach: a domestic situation to look in on. Pine Beach was a river neighborhood of about two hundred cottages that were originally developed for factory workers from Brockton, but the workers had never come. The houses were packed in cheek by jowl, with chain-link fences between them. There was only one way in and out of the neighborhood unless you traveled by water.

The call had come to me from one of the neighbors, a man I went to high school with. He must have known in an obscure manner nobody quite wished to discuss that I was responsible for the house. There had been loud arguments the previous three nights, he said, which had woken up and frightened his children. In the morning they were at it again, the two men who were living in the house. Both were clients of long standing, people my father brought in before I was working. One went by the name Udder. A name he'd chosen for himself, I didn't know why. He had run a motorcycle club out of Charleston, South Carolina. The club was getting ready to retire him over missing cargo and cash when he jumped overboard and washed up in Onset. The other man's name was Hector. An old organizer during the Chicano Movement in Oakland. He was writing a book. He had been writing a book for as long as I had been working his account, and when I got to the cottage, I saw he was at it still. There were manuscript pages everywhere. The two of them were sitting in armchairs in the middle of those stacks, facing each other across the room. In Onset, they were lovers. In their previous lives they had been practicing Catholics, of a sort. They had been together for years now. The first weekend every December, they held a Christmas party. My father moved them into the house when things were quiet one winter. They had been living in that place for a long time, happily it seemed to me, Udder doing light mechanic work and living off the money he stole from his club, and Hector working on his book. You would see them out at the movies on Cranberry Highway once in a while, at the little art house theater with wooden seats.

Their fight, if that's what it was, had been going on for days. They admitted it readily enough and apologized about the noise. Udder said they would send the neighbor a bottle of something, no hard feelings. He sounded pretty sincere about it: making amends, being sorry. It was the heat, Hector said, but his heart wasn't in it, and Udder spoke over him before he could finish the thought and said it was "that goddamn waiter."

"This is gonna kill us," he said.

They were sitting in those armchairs, neither man moving, both of them gripping the fat wooden arms and sweating into the upholstery. There weren't any fans in the room because of the pages of Hector's book. He told me about it once: a coming-of-age novel.

"He's off tonight," Hector said. "No work, enjoying himself somewhere."

"Good," Udder said. "He should enjoy himself. He's young, isn't he?"

There was a waiter they were both hung up on. It took me a while to get the story straight. A kid named Thomas. Twenty-two, with a lean build and blond hair. He was waiting tables at Picanha, a Brazilian steak house on Cranberry Highway. Udder and Hector had been drinking more than they liked to drink in public because they wanted to see him and felt obliged to order a good deal so they could give him a big tip without making things awkward for him or anyone else. I knew the kid they meant. I had seen him around town hustling. I told them to pick another restaurant to drink in and they said they would try. Thomas was leaving anyway. He was in town only for a few weeks. While I was heading out, Udder put on some music, and they said they were going to have a quiet night in. The music he put on was French. "My Way," but the original, performed by Claude François, and I figured it would go on like that between them for a few more nights, until they reached a détente, and it wouldn't really get better until the season ended and the heat broke and the waiters all cleared out of town.

LATER, I WENT TO SEE my father. His house was on a hill overlooking the harbor. In the backyard was a modest vegetable garden and some Adirondack chairs he had built himself. His friend Caterina was there. A refined, darkly freckled woman who taught health and gym at the high school and coached the girls field hockey team. They had been together for several years, but she always excused herself when I came around. She did it very courteously, without ever seeming embarrassed. My father called after her, something about a game coming up, and we sat down to talk. He wanted to tell me about her game. It was against Durfee. Durfee was a large, tough school in Fall River.

"She's under a lot of pressure," he said. "Remarkable woman, it never shows."

He was three years into semiretirement. For the good of the enterprise, that fact wasn't widely disclosed. He wasn't somebody who felt the need to stay especially busy, but he always took up new activities and people. Hobbies, you would have to call them. Woodworking, tennis, subscriptions to newsletters. Substances, sometimes. He had given up drinking liquor and taken to smoking, at first modestly, later with reckless abandon. Finally, he had settled into a daily regimen of hashish. Where he got the hash, I never asked. It wasn't the kind of thing you could buy on the corner, though I supposed he had connections all over. Those connections were still our stock-in-trade.

He had worked the Mediterranean shipping and telecom routes for just over ten years, recruiting and running agents deemed of use to American intelligence, primarily the National Security Agency, though he had been brought up by Navy intelligence and reared at a listening station in Cyprus that was shared with the CIA during the conflict years. He eventually grew tired of the work. When they wouldn't let him go home, he claimed he had forgotten how to speak the languages they trained him to speak and how to perform the jobs they counted on him doing. He was locked in a brig on a military base in the desert, somewhere in northern Morocco, and held there for just over six months, guarded by a pair of Marines who were always offering him comic books to read. He practiced a loose form of Buddhism to pass the time. I assumed that was where he started smoking hash, too, although it could have just as easily been Tangier or Beirut.

I told him something was bothering me. The Stamford kid maybe. I didn't know what.

"Ennui is natural in this line of work," he said. "Next comes the disenchantment. The trick is finding you were never enchanted in the first place. That's a peaceable solution."

The case had come in from a broker in New York, a man we worked with named Bruno.

The kid had stolen something from his employer, a private equity shop, and sold it to a competitor. What he stole, I didn't know. Probably he'd incurred some gambling debts and then been leaned on. That was the usual course. It worried me, having him around.

I had put him in a two-room cottage on Elm, north of the green. There was air-conditioning, a TV, a working DVD player, and a nice collection of films. I hoped it would be enough to keep him inside awhile. There wasn't a lot of air-conditioning in town. You would see people sleeping in their yards, in hammocks, praying for a breeze.

My father was the one who had fielded the call. He did that sometimes, wandered into the office late at night. He had a way of talking on the phone that wasn't quite in code but wasn't exactly intelligible either. Polite inquiries after family and last night's scores.

"He'll be gone soon," he said. "A few days, a week, from the sound of it."

"You didn't pick up on anything?"

"It's a flash case. You're supposed to be alert, anxious, that's why they flash it at you."

We spoke for a while about other clients. Long-term cases, the ones he still kept tabs on. We held some people for a night and others stayed in town for years. At a certain point they were no longer hiding, they were just residents. Respectable citizens, like anybody else. Like Hector and Udder, going out to the movies or to a steak house now and again.

Around sundown, I noticed he was gripping the arm of his chair. His knuckles were white. We were back around to the subject of the flash case, the kid from Stamford, whether there was anything to worry about, anything unseen. The spy's pastime, guessing at motivations, gossiping like hens, but shrouded in talk of rivalries and vices.

He thought I was onto something. Maybe the kid was hiding from us too. What of it?

"You need a wild card every now and again," he said. "A place like this, it has a proper balance. You can't have too many professionals or too many civilians, too many who want to stay or too many on their way out. Everything has to be just right for the balance to hold, and that's what you're around for. You press your thumb down on a spot, then another, and you feel for the perfect weightless point where it's all balanced."

"I don't know what that means."

"Neither do I. Stay for dinner. Any minute I'll start shaking. It's getting late, isn't it?"

His Parkinson's was mild still. That's what the doctor said. It was another kind of code.

"There's swordfish on the counter," he said. "Put it on the grill, huh?"

The swordfish was there, already seasoned. I cooked it over charcoal in the garden while he smoked some hash to beat back the tremors and give himself an appetite.

"Can you pick out the spices?" he asked.

There was coriander and cumin on the fish. A dash of rosemary.

"No," I said. "Not a clue. You're a sphinx."

He had his spices brought in, maybe with the hash. He was proud of them.

"If you're worried about the Stamford kid, pay Bruno a visit."

"I talked to him yesterday. He said the job's clean, paid in full, no flags on his end."

For several years, the dusty remnants of the Italian crime families and the somewhat more robust sprawl of the Russian mob made up our primary customer base. They always needed people moved out of the country or relocated to another region or merely shuffled around on the board. Sometimes we worked with white collars, although typically they came to us through brokers. The brokers were connected too.

In the old days, my father had worked with a lot of political types. That was how it had started. Then lines were muddied or crossed and he had begun taking in the more regular work on offer from the New York families. He always told me that it didn't matter what kind of criminal you were dealing with. We were separate from them. Whatever they had done or not done or been forced into had no bearing on our work. Our work had its own demands and justifications. It sounded like a rationale he had convinced himself of a long time before. That was something spies had a tremendous talent for. I had met a good number of them over the years; more than I knew, in all likelihood. Spies were on the lookout for a clean exit too. They farmed out the logistics.

"You've had the Stamford kid five days," my father said. "You know him better than he knows himself by now. If there were something there, you'd be able to tell me what. Instinct works for the first forty-eight hours. After that you need evidence for a hunch."

"I guess I missed that part of the hornbook."

"There's a whole other book I haven't given you yet. You know the Druze in Israel, they don't receive their bibles until they're forty. Safer that way. Weeds out the simple."

He was right. I was looking for reasons to worry. Chasing after my tail.

It was the heat, I told myself, and tried to believe it. It muddled your thinking, having the air so still. Over the harbor, the water looked like it had frozen. It hadn't frozen in winter since the cold spell after a nor'easter in 1992, but in summer it could get so calm.

"You wouldn't believe who I saw in Stop & Shop the other day," he said.

"I would, yes."

"Squeezing peaches, God help me. Nearly knocked me over, a thing like that."

He had always liked Elena. She used to buy him pastries from a bakery in New Bedford. Delicate little egg tarts that would crack open if jostled. I didn't know the name of the bakery. They wouldn't tell me. It was their secret, a language they shared.

He said to me once, only half joking, that she was an artist. It sounded like just about the highest compliment he could think to give. I had never heard him speaking about any local with that kind of admiration. Yet he hardly knew her. They had only met a half-dozen times. She usually sent the egg tarts to him with me as an intermediary. That was the kind of thing he enjoyed: breaking down a job and establishing walls and mirrors between the components. And using me as a courier, working blindly in between them.

"I saw her at Marianne's," I said. "She's been back, I don't know, a few days."

"And planning to stay awhile?"

"She says weeks, possibly. I think she was waiting for me to tell her it was a bad idea."

"Did you?"

"I didn't know what to tell her."

He thought it over a moment. "In terms of immediate safety, I'd say she's in the clear. The people whose finances she disturbed, dead and gone, lost to time. It was never all that serious to begin with, was it? You were closer to it than I was. I assumed she just wanted to go. Seemed headed that way. Some people need a little distance from home."

"Yes," I said. "She wanted to go."

"And now she wants to come back. For a visit, or longer. But you, what, object?"

"It's been a long time. She built a life for herself. In New York. A nice life."

"So you're feeling protective. Of your peace or hers?"

"I'm just wondering why she's here."

"You know why. What other reason could she have? A spirit like that can abstain only for so long. That's what this is about. She took different vows than you and I did. If she's here, she must be feeling them tugging. Vows tugging on all those stray, loose ends of whatever life she built herself in New York. How long's she been away now?"

"Seven years."

"There you go. That's when it starts to itch. Did she ever get married?"

"She was engaged."

"How long?"

"Six years."

He began to laugh. At the start, it resembled a tremor.

"That's a long time to string someone along. God bless her if she could. And now?"

"Broke it off. Recently."

"He was from money, wasn't he? Vineyard, by way of New York. That's another life to disappear into. A new name. Family like a thicket. I guess she wasn't interested in that."

"No, I guess not."

We were gossiping again. A pair of hens, clucking.

"You liked seeing her," he said. "That's good and natural. Just don't forget yourself."

"I don't know whether I liked seeing her. It was uncanny."

He nodded a few times and didn't say anything more.

His eyes were closed again. He was fighting something off, not a tremor but something worse. In moments he would freeze up, like the harbor water appeared to. Something would have to get him going again. He had described the tremors to me before and sounded lighthearted enough, but we never spoke about the other moments.

After a while he came back, smirking again. Thinking about peaches maybe.

"Let's have some music," he said.

I took out my phone and was going to play something, but he wouldn't allow it. He had an old record player and a collection of morna from Cape Verde and fado from Portugal. It was a good collection, built over a lifetime and cared for meticulously. He placed the speaker next to one of the window screens and turned up the volume. Certain notes would shake the flimsy wall he'd built to capture the view through those flimsy windows. It was how he always listened to morna, even in winter when the town went dark and quiet. He said the neighbors didn't mind, the music touched their souls, and maybe it did too. It was music for a tavern on the shore.

When we used to go on the road, my father was the one who always chose the music. Exile ballads were his favorites, his passion, whatever country they came from. We used to listen for hours on end to the cassettes he had recorded off the vinyls. It didn't matter what the client wanted to listen to. That wasn't something you could buy with the service. Listening to the songs, he would ask questions. The questions sounded absurd and irrelevant, then the next lyric would be sung and it would turn out to be responsive, as though a long, searching conversation was being conducted between two intimates who wished to reach an understanding. He could keep it up for days without getting tired of the joke. It used to drive some of the men crazy, and maybe that was why he did it. It used to drive me a little crazy too. Now, I missed it. During solitary border trips I often found myself listening to his old cassettes and repeating the old questions and thinking about the drives we had taken together. It was different, working alone. Your mind took you to all kinds of odd places.

When I was younger, in college still and figuring myself out, I put my name in for intelligence work at two different agencies, very naively and without telling anyone, least of all my father. It turned out one of his old stablemates had risen to the subdirector level, and when a flag went up on my name he wrote to my father, who wrote him back and said that I was pure, loyal, sensitive, and saw duplicity at every turn.

You would have thought that was an endorsement. Probably I didn't understand the profession. I was rejected by the agencies, and one of my professors, the one who had encouraged me in that direction, told me there was no use in pursuing it any further; I had been blackballed. It wasn't something I regretted too deeply. In fact, we used to laugh about it, my father and I, whenever it came up, which it sometimes did on those long, meandering drives home. While he drove, he would pretend to dictate a new letter to his friend, elaborating on more of my paradoxical shortcomings. Always, they were traits he shared. He could talk for tremendous amounts of time without ever losing track of you and your interest. That was his great gift, and I often missed it when I was out on the road alone, although sometimes it just felt like a subtler form of interrogation.

He was still in his yard listening to the music when I left. I could hear it a long way off.

Walking home along the beach, I kept thinking about the Stamford kid and about Elena. I came across a pack of seagulls and for some reason ran straight at them, the way a child does when he's at the beach and his mother is distracted by something. They took off in a panic. The rest of the way, they were overhead, chattering nervously.

5

Elena used to work a lot of jobs, three or four at a time. She waited tables for a while at Audrey's, a seafood and cocktail lounge at the five-mile mark on Cranberry Highway. There were plenty of shifts available and she worked most of them until the manager accused one of the other women of stealing and Elena threw a hot drink in his face. Coffee or mulled wine. They would serve mulled drinks in the fall, after the tourists left.

She grew up in Onset, but I didn't know her then. She went to a Catholic school in Fairhaven. When I met her, I was back from college and starting work with my father. That was the year the Dominicans and Haitians in Boston were at each other's throats. There was a lot to do and people to move around and family rivalries to keep straight. I was still getting used to the work. I went over to Jacobs Neck one day to see some cottages. Nobody was living there. The whole street had cleared out two years before, after a nor'easter. There was still some mold and flood damage but the cottages were mostly in fine, habitable shape. Elena took me through each one and recited the specs. She even had opinions about repairs and what ought to be done before winter if the pipes were going to survive. Jacobs Neck was a woodsy, secluded part of town and I figured that if I put either the Haitians or the Dominicans there, they wouldn't find each other. Anyway, it didn't matter. Once in Onset, grudges tended to dissipate. Everyone was headed somewhere. Back home or to someplace new. Or they would caravan up to Mattapan and take their chances, if they were feeling desperate. I took notes concerning the cottages and the repairs Elena was recommending and sketched out some floor plans. She named me a good rent and said there was an application fee. Five hundred dollars.

"Credit checks and all that," she said. "If you have cash, I'll get them started today."

Five hundred seemed steep but I understood it was for more than paperwork.

She knew who I was, the broad strokes, and what I was doing there.

My father had operated the business always as an open yet poorly understood secret. There were several reasons why, but the foremost had to do with community morale and a belief, firmly held, that if you gave people a glimpse, rather than shutting them out entirely, they would transfer some piece of themselves onto you and take pride in your work and your success. That, and Onset was a small town with a few big families. All the families received envelopes and had come to rely on that money as other industries dried up. The fishing fleet was gone. The cranberry bogs were shrinking.

The motels were still in need of warm bodies and the New England highway system ran toward Onset like rivers to a sea. That was the town's one piece of good fortune. The highways would maintain for it an air of convenience and proximity, but once you got off the ramps, you might as well have been on another continent, it was so removed.

I gave her the cash. At that time, I still thought the job was about handing out bills and collecting favors. It was a week before I figured out that she didn't represent the homeowners. She wasn't a real estate agent at all. She was just squatting out in Jacobs Neck and saw me coming in and took a chance. It was a scam. Not a bad one either. I was too embarrassed to tell anybody what had happened. It was a learning experience.

I didn't see her again for a month or so. When I did, she was waiting tables at Audrey's, where the old manager had been fired and a new one hired, who had asked her back. She was really flying. Her section seemed to have every table in the restaurant. The other waiters were props for her to work with. It was impressive, like watching a good athlete who had trained in a very disciplined fashion and now could improvise and commit herself to aesthetic concerns. She bought me a Shirley Temple and said no hard feelings.

"You know a lot about houses," I said.

She shrugged. It was a sudden, graceful gesture. "My father was a general contractor."

"No, he wasn't."

"No, I guess not. So, you looked me up?"

"I asked around."

"I cleared out of Jacobs, just in case. Thought you might come for a refund."

She had an easy smile. She was enjoying herself and I was glad.

"Think of it like a bet," she said. "We had a fair wager, you and I. You, walking through the world betting nobody was going to rob you. Me, on the other side of it. Both of us with eyes open. Sportsmanship is a lost art, don't you think? It's all about perspective."

"I don't want the money."

"Good, how about giving me a ride then? My car's in the shop."

I hung around drinking Shirley Temples until her shift was over.

On the way back, driving into the village, she asked if I had ever met a Kennedy.

"A real one," she said. "Dyed in the wool, doomed from the cradle."

"Not that I know of."

She was thinking over something very carefully. Deciding whether to tell me.

"Someone was in the restaurant earlier," she said, "pretending to be a Kennedy."

"How do you know he was pretending?"

Another shrug. "I just know, that's all. You smell it. I can anyway. The other girls couldn't. They were talking about him all night, and Tim at the bar ripped up his tab."

"Why'd he do that?"

"Maybe he thought it was bad luck to charge a Kennedy."

We drove in silence for a while and talked about other things. The jobs she was working and who her family was. I knew some of it already. Her father had been a professional drunk and a gambler who people used to call the duke or the count, depending on when he introduced himself and how much of it they remembered. Supposedly he won a Brockton city bus off a driver once, in a hand of five-card stud, and drove the thing to California. I had heard the story told before but never thought about a family waiting for him at home. She didn't tell me the bus story but she mentioned her father in passing, and I could hear in her voice that she knew I knew.

After I let her out, she walked around the car and leaned against the window frame. Her hair was pinned up. She was wearing a pair of old running sneakers. Bone-white Nikes with the waffle soles.

"We should try the Kennedy thing sometime," she said.

"Sure. You want to do it at Audrey's or take it on the road?"

"Who's going to tell us we're not? Anyhow, think it over. You're a good sport, Jack."

I watched her go in. Later, I found out it wasn't her place. She just slipped out the back.

6

spent most of Monday evening dealing with two Romanian brothers who had made their way into town twelve days prior and were staying in a cottage near Stonebridge. We talked through their options for quite a long time. Hours maybe. I got the impression they were talking merely to hear the sounds. That they had already decided what they wanted to do. Probably I would arrive at the cottage in a day or a week, and they would be gone without my having to deliver them anywhere. As we talked, they kept finishing each other's sentences. It was disarming because they had similar voices but different accents. One had learned his English in America, in Brooklyn. The other studied in Scotland. Both were Romanian; there was no mistaking them for native speakers. Still, it was odd hearing them hand off the conversation so fluidly, nearly the same voice coming out but the inflections and rhythms changing from one thought to the next. And hearing how perfectly natural it was for them. They were twins in fact.

I drove straight from the Romanians to Monk Teller's on Lavender Road, near the Gateway marsh. In front, they served lobster rolls without any mayonnaise. In the back room was a nightly card game. Quite a few of our clients played. There were always card games going in Onset. It could feel some nights like either a prison or a casino town, depending on your mood, but the reality is, people, in particular those on the run, need to keep busy. There wasn't always a common language or sentiment among them, but they could play cards and get along for a few hours and pass the time.

A great deal of the local economy was formed around time—how to use it up, how to save it, how to conceive of its passage. For every new arrival we ran, it often seemed there were three or four or five civilians sniffing around to learn what they could offer in the way of distraction or diversion. Drugs, cards, food, sex, companionship, fishing equipment. Sometimes clients would show up at the playground and bet on pickup basketball. There was always some local around who would give them a line. They would find a kid to hold the money during game play. You couldn't let it get out of hand, or if you did, you needed to make sure their exits had been paid in full, up front.

Monk's was one of the more respectable games in town. Small tables, middling stakes. It took my eyes a moment to adjust to the smoke and the near darkness of the room. There was only one table going, with five players, all of them wearing baseball caps. Another four were watching the action, such as it was. At the center was Elena, dealing.

I had forgotten she used to deal at Monk's place. Twice a week, Monday and Wednesday nights. I would give her rides to the New Bedford docks every other weekend. She always carried a leather satchel. I got the feeling she was moving money for somebody back then but never asked. She didn't have a car. I figured that out about a month after we met, a half-dozen rides later. She told me she didn't know how to drive at all, so I took her down to the beach parking lot one night and showed her how the clutch and the gears worked. She picked it up so quickly, so smoothly, it made me wonder whether she was just having some fun with me, seeing how far she could carry the story. She had a good way with cards. An even better way with gamblers. Her childhood had been spent dragging her father out of back rooms, at Monk's and other places.

I was there to check in on one client in particular, a guy named Devers who shuttled between New York, Hartford, and Boston, depending on what was needed. He came to us every summer. He told his crew he was in the DR; Onset was his holiday. He liked to do a little coke and drink and gamble. How word of his whereabouts never got back to his guys in Washington Heights, I couldn't have told you. Maybe it did, but they respected his time off and the effort that went into the charade. He liked poker especially, but was terrible at it, and would insist on being extended lines of credit, which Monk didn't have the means or inclination to give. In quiet moments, Devers used to ask that I come by the game now and again to check on him, his losses, and to remind him about the credit lines. He was a decent guy and always thinking ahead, taking precautions against himself. The same as he knew he needed a vacation and to be circumspect about it. He was pretty far into the evening by the time I got there. Normally, I might have tried to pull him out, but Elena gave me a nod and I took it to mean that she understood the situation and would look after it, so I sat down to watch.

"We're gonna keep that pot moving," she said, clearing the table, setting up a new hand. Her sleeves were rolled. Her eyes suggesting a smile. "Stirred pot's a happy pot."

Her family was one of those large old Azorean clans who seem to have nothing particular holding them together except a few scattered fables about their seafaring ancestors and an intense, almost-impossible darkness around the brow and hairlines. Cousins and uncles and aunts, always passing by one another on the street like strangers. Elena hadn't lived with her mother since she was fifteen. Her father died quietly one winter, drowned somewhere off India Point in Providence. An accident.

The summer we met, I was taking classes at Southern New England School of Law. Something my father had dreamed up. We already had a spy; a lawyer might come in handy too.

Besides waiting tables at Audrey's and dealing cards at Monk's on Mondays and Wednesdays, she kept books for the water park on Cranberry Highway and an insurance agency in New Bedford that mostly dealt with fishermen. There were other jobs, too, but you couldn't pin her down on them. And then she carried those satchels every other week. She was a hustler, a worker. Her mind was balancing numbers, figuring odds. Skills inherited from her father maybe? But she was better with it.

I used to pick her up wherever she was. I was always changing cell phones back then. She would write down the numbers on the backs of matchbooks, then burn them later.

Driving, we took back roads and let time stretch out. Off the highway, you were in country. Marshland and cranberry bogs and dirt roads that petered out into salt lakes.

She liked hearing about cases we were studying at school. How they fit together and amounted to something almost mystical: the idea of a common law, rules unspoken, decisions gleaned from custom, reason, and half-imagined histories nobody could verify.

She used to say that after I was done, when I had my law degree, I could write my own ticket. It sounded like something your grandmother would tell her friends about you over canasta. She meant it though. She wanted to get out. She was studying languages. She spoke Portuguese, Spanish, Italian, and French. She was working on Arabic and Mandarin. If there had been more people to practice with, she'd have mastered them already. She told me she was going to start her own language school. She would train diplomats. All you had to do was get a government contract and they would send you all their people and you'd be guaranteed an income. People wanted conversation, she said. It didn't matter what language they spoke or what they did for a living, they wanted someone to talk to. If you could provide it they'd give you everything they had.

We would talk quite a lot about Onset, as well. Elena had picked up a different version of the town's history. It was from her I first heard about the wreckers, alternately called moon-cussers, who led ships into the rocks, then plundered what they could from the damage. They could operate only on dark nights and raved at the moon for getting in the way of their scores. Later, the Azoreans were celebrated bootleggers and smugglers. Every fishing town in the world has smuggler stories, just like they have dope and working women and suicides when the boats are in dry dock.

Gambling, too, was always on, long before Monk Teller's back room. Before it was a necessary pastime for the people my father brought in. It was wilder in the old days. She told me once about a wire scheme. It had to do with results from grass-run horse tracks coming in from Great Britain and France, which could be intercepted over the old Cape lines and used to build a two-minute advantage over bettors off the coast. It was a decades-old scam but she talked about it admiringly and like it was fresh and she had seen it operating and held the betting slips in her own hands.

I always wondered how much of it she was embellishing or inventing. She told me I wouldn't understand. I couldn't because my father had kept me apart from that side of the town. I asked what that meant. I thought of myself as an apprentice outlaw then, because of the trade I had started to learn and everything I had seen my father do and sometimes went alongside him for when I was young. She said I was no outlaw. I was the ferryman. The words were whispered from the passenger seat, difficult to hear with the windows down. I didn't think she meant any offense, just the opposite.

She was always running some kind of scam. The more complicated, the better. For a while she got into trouble with a group backed by some people in the North End. It had to do with car insurance. I really didn't know how she got mixed up in it. They sent guys to look for her. Big, drowsy men wearing round-toed shoes in the middle of summer, driving Buicks through the village center. Asking my father what he knew about her, where to find her. I used to worry sometimes that one day she would need our services, but she managed to make it right, or she just fed them a story and moved on to the next mark. She always talked about putting together a good, clean job and then leaving. By job, I gathered that she meant something illicit, but she never said as much.

In the end, it always struck me as funny that Elena's way out was law school. She used an old family name from her mother's side, Souza, when she filled out the applications. She might have gone to college first but didn't see the point. The transcripts and diploma were forged but the LSAT scores were real, apparently. She took books out of the library and practiced the test with them and did well enough that she could go anywhere she liked. She chose Columbia, followed by a corporate firm in Midtown. A life, clean and simple. That was seven years before. In that time, as far as I knew, she never stepped foot in Onset. I had figured she never would. That was fine. It was the way she wanted it.

But then, she came back. Without any warning or preliminaries, for reasons unknown.

She looked happy at the card table. Every now and again she would crack her knuckles.

"It's twenty to watch," she said.

The players turned. I had been there over an hour. It seemed they were just noticing.

"I'm not watching," I said. "I thought this was where you wait for lobster rolls."

"Play a few hands. We'll make room."

One of the men at the table scooted over. He was noisy doing it and seemed put out.

Elena nodded toward the open spot. Her face had hardened slightly.

"Well," she said. "It's all yours."

"Another time."

"All right, keep that pot moving, fellas. Another time, the man said. He likes to watch."

The game broke up around two thirty. She managed to keep all five players in funds, even Devers, who kept excusing himself very deferentially to use the restroom, which was cornered off by cheap plywood walls. Inside, he would do a few lines. Then he'd be seized by a sneezing fit, and just when he got rid of it, the coughing would start. Once, at around midnight, he vomited. The sound rattled straight through the plywood and into the game room, so there was no ignoring it. He came back out with his shirt smoothed and tucked and his hair fixed and his face washed, and he summoned some deep well of dignity, pulling out his chair and lowering himself into it with a demure smile and a word of thanks to the other players, who had waited for him, and to Elena.

Normally, in that state, he would have gone bust hours before, but Elena was bottom-dealing. She kept him in it and knew how to buoy his spirit and the spirits of the others.

It was the banter that did it. Every card game I'd ever seen, and I had seen more than I cared to, fell eventually into silence as the players reckoned with their hopes and losses. Occasionally some loudmouth would try to needle his opponents. I had never seen a dealer keep up a conversation like that, but she managed it without being intrusive. She knew when to keep quiet, too, only nobody ever seemed to want that from her. You got the feeling they were playing just to spend some time with her. For the conversation.

After the game, she asked me about Devers. "He was your client, wasn't he?"

The room had cleared out, and we were turning chairs over onto the tables.

"Three of them were mine," I said. "He was the one I was worried about."

She asked a few more questions and I told her what she wanted to know.

"I liked the way he came back to the table," she said. "Brushing himself down."

"Like a racehorse."

"Exactly. That lather on him. That sheen. Christ, I liked the way he did that." After a pause, she looked at me sadly. "Don't you ever play?"

"Sure, once in a while."

"When?"

"Casino night at the school. They do it every year before Christmas."

She didn't think that was funny. It wasn't meant to be. It was only the truth.

"No," she said. "You like to watch. You gather souls. I do that, too, but I ante up first."

"You play a lot of cards in the city?"

"Never. I wasn't sure I could manage it anymore."

"That deal? They didn't care."

"Was I so clumsy they noticed?"

I thought about it before answering. "Only Devers noticed."

"That's right. Only Devers. Good man, that one. He was an individual, Jack."

It was an old theory of hers. How few individuals you encountered, and how important it was to recognize and appreciate them as they passed you by. Something we used to discuss on those drives. For some reason, I pretended not to remember, and she let it go.

7

It was a Thursday and I drove straight to the playground and changed in the car. There was already a game going. I hated joining late. You wanted to be around for the first moments, when everybody was shooting quietly and you had the numbers to play but nobody would say the word to get things going. Or somebody would, but it wouldn't take straightaway. Those were the moments to savor. After that, it began to spoil some.

The lights were on, which meant Tommy was back. He had missed only a week. You could tell he had been gone from the way he was running the sidelines, tearing ass up and down the court and calling for the ball when it made no sense to pass it to him. Laughing when he didn't get it, patting himself on the chest, like it was his fault, the overeagerness—like he recognized it in himself and couldn't contain it or didn't want to.

The Stamford kid was playing too. Anybody could play. You only had to show up and hit a free throw or wait around. I didn't like seeing him out of the house, a flash case, but I wasn't his jailer. I would do the best for him I could. If he wanted to show his face to a lot of potential informants, that was his business and he might end up dead or in prison. There was a calculus to it, and everybody had to do the numbers for themselves.

His team won the game, and when I got on, I decided to guard him.

Physically, we were alike in many ways. I had maybe fifteen pounds on him, and I wanted to squash out some of his quickness. Whenever he cut, I went with him and around the screens, which were lazy pickup screens of no particular consequence. When he had the ball, I put a hand on his hip. That was enough to keep him off balance.

He didn't say anything about the defense. He just dug in and ran harder. He lost me once and made for the rim, but the pass was off target. Reaching after it awkwardly, he ended up on Danny Trahearne's back. Danny had a big body with a lot of back to get lost on, and for a moment it seemed like the kid might tumble over and go headfirst into the blacktop, but Danny stopped, hunched, and the kid slid down him onto his feet.

It was like watching a bullfight. A disaster conjured up, and then it was gone, vanished.

"You okay?" I asked.

The game had stopped. It was ball out at the top, though there hadn't been a foul call. Sometimes the game stops like that for no particular reason. You've had a brush up against death and it takes a beat to recover.

"Fine," the kid said. "Let's just play, all right."

The next play he took me into the post. The ball was no-where near us, but he dug his shoulder into my chest and tried moving me toward the block. It was an angry action and slightly wild. Old men played that way, working through their memories and disappointments. He didn't have the weight for it, and I slid a hip around him and knocked him off bal-ance again. He was getting frustrated, and I thought for a mo-ment he might take a swing at me, but the hatred was just a flare. He went cold again, almost lifeless, and we were back to running off screens and canceling each other out while the game went on around us and the sun went down into the marsh.

Afterward, he came with us to Alphonse's. Tommy asked him along. They'd been playing together all night. Sometimes you form bonds with people who do different things than you do on the court, somebody who doesn't mind rebounding or who makes a few pocket passes. It's a kind of humbleness, really. A recognition of shortcomings and a way of welcoming the world to fill them in. Tommy invited him to sit down at our table.

He wanted to know whether the kid had played in college.

"You got some bullshit D3 moves," he said.

"No," the kid said. "Just high school."

It was a lie. He had played in college, a Division 3 school, like Tommy guessed.

The kid was looking at me, maybe to see whether I approved

of the deception. He had an odd quality about him. Something uncanny. The night before, I'd seen him out of the house and had decided then, too, not to say anything. He had been down by the beach, sitting at the end of a dock, with his legs swinging over the end, looking like an overgrown teenager whose parents had taken him along for one final family vacation before breaking the news about a divorce. I might have delivered a lecture about the seriousness of the situation he found himself in and how it wasn't safe to go around wherever he pleased, carrying on stupidly. Probably I should have, but I let it go instead.

I had only ever dealt with a handful of flash cases.

Somebody must have made the arrangement for him. The expenditure was pretty significant: a full exfiltration, new documents. I had been working up papers off and on throughout the week. He would have an engineering degree and a Canadian passport.

"I always wanted to walk on somewhere," Tommy said. "Some big fucking program, walk on and just bust asses at practice and whoop it up during games. One of those guys who gets on in the tournament when you're down, you know? Fucking charity case, those white boys they put in when it's all over. I thought I could've done it okay."

The kid nodded. "I get that," he said. "It's good to put in the work."

"Exactly," Tommy said. "The work's fucking everything. Most guys don't know that."

"What, are you coaching now?" I asked.

He looked hurt or like he had forgotten I was there. "I'm just talking," he said.

"What about you guys?" the kid asked. "Any of you play college?"

"Sure, Jack did," Tommy said.

"Oh yeah?"

"Harvard. Ivy League bids. Didn't make the tournament though."

The kid looked at me. Tommy seemed to be waiting for something too.

I went inside for a while and sat at the bar. It was a long block of wood nailed into legs and looked like something you might build in your basement and then forget about for several years. There were a few banners hanging above the bottles, commemorating summer festivals. Alphonse was in there. He was talking to someone, maybe one of his relatives. They were speaking in Portuguese and didn't look in my direction. I already had the drink and they probably knew that I was only hiding out for a few minutes.

One of the photographs hanging on the wall behind the bar was of Tommy at fifteen, wearing boxing gloves that looked too large for him. It must have been taken when he won the Police Athletic League title. Somehow, he had never mentioned it was hanging here, though we had been in Alphonse's café countless times throughout the years.

I had a strange thought just then: What if I brought Tommy into the business? What if I made him a partner? I could teach him the work. Anyone could learn. It was a preposterous idea, but I was enjoying it and I sat in there for what felt a very long time, thinking through how it might work: how I would tell him, and if my father would agree, when we would begin, how long it would take before he could be let out on his own. I figured he would enjoy it for a while. It might suit him perfectly fine. And then later, if he stopped enjoying it, he could simply leave. He would know just how to do it.

WHEN I WENT BACK OUTSIDE, Elena was in my chair. Her legs were kicked up on the rail that separated the tables from the sidewalk, and she looked awfully comfortable. I thought it would be a shame to disturb her in any way and I ought to slip out the side.

"Get over here," she said. "You're always sneaking off. A busman's holiday."

"Trying to stay loose," I said. "In case anyone wants another game."

"You weren't loose a day in your life. Come on, sit down with us."

She was telling Tommy and the kid a story. It was a story you might tell to a good friend or to somebody with whom you shared a lot of mutual acquaintances. I tried remembering whether she and Tommy were related somehow. It was possible. She had one of the beer bottles from the bucket and was running the wet glass across the back of her neck.

"Jack, you're going to take me somewhere," she said. "Tonight, please."

"I don't have my car."

"The Jeep's right over there. I'm not blind. We don't need a car, so quit the excuses."

I tried a few more but she wouldn't accept any of them.

"I can take you," Tommy said. "I don't have any plans."

"That's generous of you," she said and turned to me. "You see how courtesy works?"

"Where do you want to go?" Tommy asked.

She shook her head. "I can't say it in front of Jack. He'll take off again."

"Come on," he said. "Let's go. I'll change at home. Ten minutes and I'm ready."

He was standing up and there was a fine, sheer confidence about him that was almost like sweat. No one said anything. I couldn't remember ever having seen a man so confident in something like that, and when he sat back down it was like watching a tree fall. Elena was watching it too. We all were. He started peeling the label from his bottle. I had never seen him do that either. He was very neat and always swept ashes off tabletops before sitting down.

"I'm gonna get out of here," he said when he was done with the label. "Fuck it."

He said it to no one in particular. I didn't like seeing him that way, but there was nothing to do about it.

I put down some money and went with her. She said we were going by boat.

"Whose boat?" I asked.

"That's the fun part," she said. "Do you know how to hot-wire a transmission?"

After we left, I looked back and saw the kid still sitting at the table, alone now. He seemed happy enough. The other tables were full and he was watching them on the sly.

Tommy had gotten up and left, or maybe he had only gone inside to the bar.

8

We didn't need to steal anything. She had the keys to a twenty-five-foot whaler called the *Anna Darling*. It had a fat offshore hull and a lounge in the transom. I took care of the rigging while she warmed the engine and made jokes about what they did to boat thieves in small towns in New England. They strung them up from piers, she said, and let gulls peck at their guts. They greased them up and dropped them into the bay next to buoys and watched them try to climb up the platform, sliding back in, over and over.

She was having a good time and steered us out of the harbor very smoothly without having to check the channels. A storm had come through the week before and shifted some of the sandbars, but they didn't give her any trouble and we were into the bay within a few minutes. The air out there was cooler. There were great flocks of gulls riding the wind up and down, and using the moonlight to look for clams near the shore.

"Where are we dumping the body?" I asked.

"Whose body?"

"Whichever one you have in here. I wish you'd taken Tommy as an accomplice."

She ramped up the gas and it was too loud to talk.

It was fine and good to be on the water, and I was beginning to think we were just joyriding. I almost never went anywhere by boat. The days when you could keep the Coast Guard in your pocket were gone, and there was also Joint Base Cape Cod hiding in the tall grass between Bourne and Sandwich. They were responsible for air cover on distress signals from Bar Harbor to Montauk and out onto the North Atlantic shelves. They flew patrols regularly and had drones too. You would have to be crazy to try to hide from the military on the water. On the highways, in a car, you looked like everybody else.

She took us to shore by Goose Neck. It was a narrow peninsula off the southern edge of Pocasset that split like a wishbone a half mile into the bay. From the street it looked like a modest grove of oak and scrub pine that petered out into jetty strings, but from the water you could see the houses with their gabled roofs. It was an old Cape settlement and the families there knew one another from the days of private trains from Boston, Labor Day regattas, platform tennis. I'd never heard of a house there going on sale. They were passed down through families, and if there were lawsuits among the heirs, they were settled out of court. The land gave an impression of radical stability, like it had been driven into sheer rock by an ancient, prosperous people with unknown tools.

"You see that house down there?" Elena asked. "With the lights? There's a party."

She took us toward the bank and cut the engine.

The house was an old captain's cottage that faced the bay over a sharp drop of about twenty feet. There was a stone staircase carved into the hillside. A lush lawn rolled toward the house. It was peppered with oak trees, onto which the lights had been strung.

There were forty or fifty people on the lawn. In the darkness, it was hard to be certain.

I got the impression that Elena knew the people who lived there and might have been invited to the party herself. We idled about fifty yards from the house and you could hear voices on the wind and the sound of glassware being collected by caterers.

"Friends of yours?" I asked.

"Colleagues," she said. "A partner at my firm owns the place. Frank Paulson."

"What's he like? Salt of the earth?"

"He's an old sweater you think you've thrown away. His wife's lovely, but you can't get rid of her either. I suppose that's why clients like him. You always know he'll carry on. Brings in billable hours by the truckload. Doesn't work them himself but he backs the truck up for all the associates. I'm his favorite."

It sounded like there was a great deal more to it, so I kept quiet and waited.

"He's a litigator," she said. "But all he really does is work people's taxes. Tells them what they can get away with and what they can't. Always delivers it to them as a percentage. Park some money over here and there's a twenty-one percent chance they come looking for it. Eight percent chance they actually fight you on it. Three percent chance they win. He talks like that over dinner and serves the wines himself. Picks out the bottle and pours and never spills a drop. He's making it all up. The percentages don't mean a thing. But the clients listen to him. They like the way he orders the wines."

The wind was picking up some and we rode the waves up and down. The gulls came over to see what we were doing but gave up soon enough and went back to their rocks.

"He holds on to things sometimes," she said. "Things a bank prefers not to have or the client doesn't want to declare. He's very trustworthy that way. Doesn't ask unnecessary questions and doesn't find all that much to be necessary. A consummate lawyer, perfectly dispassionate and a little brave. He has a client, somebody who's asked him for a favor. They're always doing that. This summer he's holding on to some diamonds."

"I thought you said the law was boring in New York."

"It is," she said. "It's fucking awful, Jack."

She went into the hold beneath the helm and came out with something in her hand.

"What are you doing?" I asked.

"They've got security, don't you think? Private, most likely. Let's see them."

She aimed the flare gun toward open bay and fired it. The light flashed across the water and skimmed the surface before drowning in a cloud of smoke. It was downwind, and at first there was no reaction from the shore. Twenty seconds later, two men started down the staircase. The footing there was steep and uneven, and they had to take it cautiously.

From the dock they looked around, and one of them turned on a flashlight.

I didn't think either of them was armed.

"They don't see us," Elena said.

We were hidden by darkness, or luck.

Up above, the party was carrying on. Glasses clinking and somebody laughing, drunk.

When the security men were gone, she started the engine. The wind was with us and the bay was narrow there, only a few miles across to Onset. There weren't any boats on the water until we reached the inner harbor, where we saw a flat-bottomed party boat outside the marina. A woman at the edge of the deck waved to us as we passed them by.

"I'm going to take those diamonds," Elena said. "I don't fucking care anymore, Jack."

She eased into a slip, and we tied up the ropes. The knots she tied were quite intricate. When that was done, she dropped the keys through an open window at the harbormaster's shed. There was nobody inside. In the dark, a radio was playing quietly.

"What do you think?" she asked. "Not a bad job, is it?"

"I wouldn't know. Any particular reason why you've decided to do it?"

"Because it's there to be done. You know it, Jack. Why do you ask a question like that?"

"I thought you were content."

"Where, in New York?"

"With your life. All of it. There are easier ways to break off an engagement, you know."

"That's not what this is about."

"All right."

"I mean it, Jack. It's not about any of that."

"I just figured you were happy. That's all I meant."

"Look, I didn't ask to work at a firm with a guy like Paulson. I didn't ask for him to be bent. It turns out, they all are. Maybe I knew it from the beginning. I could smell it on them. All of them. They're bent so far, they're turned around straight again. That's the law. They get their names on libraries when they're done, and in the meantime, they gorge on dinners on somebody else's dime, and when the bill comes due nobody quibbles. Clients pay it happily. Everyone's in on it. What kind of life is that? I'm supposed to just live it for fifty years without any chance of getting caught? I need something more than that. I need skin in the game. I thought you understood all that."

She sounded hurt. Disappointed at having to explain herself.

"How are you going to take them?" I asked.

"Don't," she said. "Don't do that. I won't be fucking humored."

"All right. It's none of my business."

We sat there for a time, maybe five or six minutes, pretending that I hadn't gotten on the boat with her—that she hadn't come to get me, and I hadn't gone along as willingly as ever.

"You only have to conceive of a thing as yours," she said. "That's what a good theft is."

"A matter of conception?"

"Once you've got it, a gravity begins to accumulate. It's lovely, actually."

"What does the gravity do?"

"It clarifies your thinking, to start."

"And then?"

"A heightened sensitivity arrives. That's when you begin to plan."

"Ah, that's when you start to plan. I see now."

"Cut it out, Jack. I'm trying to tell you what it's like."

"I know, I'm sorry."

"I want you to feel it. It's a good job. You could feel it, if you wanted to."

"I guess that's the problem."

"You know what I think? You were waiting for me to come back. For seven years."

"I was. Don't you remember? Spraying perfume on car seats, pining away."

"I'll bet you did too. You're a romantic. You pretend to be such a hard case."

"When did I ever pretend that?"

"All the time. You don't even know. What you do, Jack, it's ugly work. It really is."

"I drive people around. I'm the ferryman, remember?"

"Don't you ever want something more? Something you can pour yourself into." She stopped and bit her lip. "Forget it. If you really don't understand, just forget it. Let's go."

We got up and walked over to a small kitchen on Melville Lane. It was an Argentine place. They served drinks in carafes shaped like penguins, and it had something to do with Eva Perón. The owner made a remark about the shoes I was wearing. I was still in my basketball gear from earlier. Elena chatted with the woman for a while and apologized about my sneakers and asked her about the penguins and about Eva Perón.

9

That weekend, on Sunday morning, I made a run to Montreal. In the mountains, in New Hampshire, the air got thin and cool and the only radio signals that would come in were from a college station out of Burlington and another that played bluegrass without interruption. The client was a guy from New York who had robbed a poker game in Brighton Beach. He had robbed one of the same Russians who had hired him, and the same man was paying for him to go to Belarus by way of Montreal. It was a vortex of old rivalries, sleights, and moves on unknown territories that nobody except the Russians wanted any part of. I didn't try to understand. It wasn't necessary. The Russians never needed any identity work done. They only wanted their men cooled off and shipped out and that was the end of it. His name was Vasily. He was drinking all the way up the mountains and into Vermont, skirting the lake. I thought he might get drunk and start talking about lakes at home, but he was a hard, quiet man who kept only to his bottle and listened to all those fiddles and banjos.

We crossed the border out of New York, on reservation land. The reservation straddled another lake and that was how the guide wanted to cross. On the other shore, we changed for a truck. I drove the rest of the way into the city and made my way back down the tribal routes later that evening. It felt like a different season up there, a season I'd never experienced before, not summer or fall but something else entirely. The guide I hired, a kid I had worked with several times and liked a good deal, told me they had a word for it, the high summer season, but he couldn't tell me its name because it was sacred and I was an outsider, a stranger who corrupted their youth and kept them from lacrosse. We were joking around, having fun.

I always enjoyed the drive home. Every client was a weight and when you were free of one it felt like flying, no matter how many others were still strapped to you. They were back home, sitting around motel rooms and cottages, waiting patiently or less so. The waiting was the dangerous part, and you had to remind them sometimes of the life they had chosen. You would talk around the subject, vaguely, as though there was a romance to it. In my experience, nearly all career criminals think of themselves romantically. The dabblers and civilians are the ones you have to watch out for. They came to us on referral from lawyers, and sometimes they thought I was their lawyer too.

It was after midnight when I got home. I parked by the

school and walked the rest of the way. The car wasn't mine and by the end of the week it would have new plates and a new life somewhere in the Southwest, just like the Russian would be in Belarus. Everything was on the move. It was satisfying work if you looked at it from an angle.

I had recorded the Red Sox game and listened to all those hours of bluegrass to keep from finding out the score. They were in Cleveland for the weekend, a city I'd never been to. The game was a national broadcast and none of the voices were familiar. I was thinking about falling asleep on the couch when the door handle turned and banged the dead bolt. I dropped down to the floor and looked around for a weapon but there wasn't one. It was Elena. She was out on the porch, looking through the window like somebody who had locked herself out many times before.

She was with an older man: distinguished, tan, curious. I let them in.

"I want to introduce you," she said. "The two of you. I'm making an introduction."

The older gentleman came forward to shake my hand. He looked like he might have felt embarrassed but had too much poise to indulge it. He was holding himself very rigidly, like an old soldier who doesn't have the back for it any longer but still has the memory. He was a handsome man with silver at the temples and his sleeves rolled up.

"Pleased to meet you," he said. "I hope we haven't intruded."

"Jack never sleeps," Elena said. "He's a twenty-four-hour diner. Coffee and donuts."

"Still, it's very late."

"This is Javi," she said. "His full name is incredible. You wouldn't believe it."

Javi shook hands warmly. Two slow pumps. His manners were extravagant.

"Elena and I, we've only just met," he said. "She finds me exotic. It won't last, I'm sure."

"Why not?" I asked.

"It's the way of nature," he said. "Our impressions deteriorate, like all matter."

She rubbed his back gently. Neither of them seemed too sorry about the proposition.

"It's Javier Jose Cardoso Davila de Andrade, el Vizconde de Triacastela," she said. "It used to be longer, but he's shed a few titles over the years. It's the way of nature, he claims. You have to pry the names out of him. Jack, haven't you got anything to drink?"

"What would you like?"

"Oh, whatever's lying around. We haven't woken you, have we?"

"That's all right. I wasn't sleeping. I was watching a game."

"We came by earlier—a more respectable hour, nine or so—on our way to La Vache. Where were you? I wanted you and Javi to meet and now you've put me in this awkward position, making a half-ass introduction at one in the goddamn morning."

I took some wine from the fridge and told them about the run, only I made it a different route and a different city. Nearly everything about it was different except the length of time I had been gone, and in the newer version, there was still the station playing all that bluegrass.

"Javi loves music," Elena said. "That's why he's here. So he claims."

"I haven't claimed any expertise," he said. "Only an appreciation."

"Of anything in particular?" I asked.

"That's an interesting question," he said. "I tend to think not. A general appreciation seems more appropriate. But your town has quite an impressive musical tradition. In fact, I own several recordings made right here in Onset, at your festival."

"You should swap records with my father."

"I would like that very much."

He made a small bowing gesture. It was done with his chin because we were sitting.

I wondered where she had found him. She always had a collection around her, and they were no different than records or books, only some had manners and poise and gray around their temples and others were boys on the way to the Cape, drinking light beers.

She and Javi had spent some portion of the evening at La Vache, it seemed. On Sundays, musicians who made money on Fridays and Saturdays singing at restaurants and bars went to La Vache and played for one another. Some of them passed around a basket and put money into it while others took it out. Later in the summer many would play the festival, and in the meantime, they put together jobs however they could.

"Is the title real?" I asked. "You're from Spanish Galicia?"

"It's a title of no consequence," he said. "My family hasn't been in Spain for some time, but when families are away, they become more jealous of their heirlooms and claims. They live in Venezuela now, my relatives. Perhaps they will leave there and become Venezuelans rather than Spaniards. You can never know how these things will evolve."

"Tell him how you got here," Elena said.

He looked at her indulgently. He was maybe fifty or fifty-five. He was dressed in a younger man's jeans with a burnt-orange belt that matched his leather driving loafers.

"It's not such an interesting story as you believe," he said.

"Sure it is. And Jack's the mayor, he has a right to know."

"Is that so?" he said to me. "I wasn't aware. That's very interesting."

"She's teasing you," I said. "Or me. One of us."

"You're the only one with a title," she said to Javi. "Go on, tell him."

While I poured more wine in the kitchen, he told us a version of what had brought him to Onset. It wasn't only the music. He had been on his way to Wellfleet and stopped first in Onset hoping to find some records. He was going to stay with friends of his, a couple of psychiatrists from New York, on the Cape. They always held a party over the Fourth of July weekend and some of their close friends stayed on at the house for another week or two. Javi was meant to be one of them, but when he was in Onset, he went for breakfast at the Tremont Diner and saw a news broadcast from Boston and there was a picture of his friends, the two psychiatrists. The wife had been murdered and the husband was arrested for it. The police found her body washed up in the dunes.

Javi told the story very dryly, like he was relaying only what was reported on the news.

"My God," Elena said. "It's inconceivable, isn't it?"

She seemed very moved, as though it were the first time she were hearing about it.

"They're holding your friend at Barnstable County Correctional." I said. "A forty-minute drive without traffic."

Javi nodded gravely. "I don't think I wish to visit him," he said. "No, I don't think so."

"So Javi decided to stay," Elena said. "In Onset, listening to sorrowful music."

"I couldn't go on to Wellfleet," he said. "You're familiar with the town?"

"Yes," I said. "It's where the psychiatrists go in summer."

"An enclave, yes. New York would be almost as bad. Here, I don't know anyone."

"Except me," Elena said. "And now I've introduced the two of you."

He made another bow, this time to her. "It's very kind of you to take an interest."

After the second glass of wine, the story was still terrible, but it was further away, dissolving like a family secret, and we got back to talking about music and opened another bottle. Javi was awfully sorry about the imposition, coming by so late. He mentioned it twice as he got drunker and said he wanted to get us something to eat.

"Yes," Elena said. "Jack and I need to talk. You could get us something, couldn't you?"

"Do you eat ham?"

He was asking the both of us. It seemed a very ordinary question.

"Jamón ibérico," he said. "I know a man. He has the jamón. It's de bellota. Acorns."

"It's really not necessary," I said.

"It would be my great pleasure," he said. "Please allow me."

He stood up and bowed again and I walked him onto the porch. His car was parked along the curb outside the house, by the stairs to the beach. It was a silver Mercedes convertible with the top down and there was dew on the hood and probably on the leather seats. The car made a strong impression and I thought about advising him against leaving it out on curbs that way, but didn't want to disabuse him of any illusions. He seemed to me somehow childlike, despite everything that had happened.

"There's only one thing," he said. "It's rather far, I think. Nearly Providence."

He meant the jamón ibérico de bellota. The man he was going to see to get the ham.

I told him it was all right, he didn't have to go, but he said he'd be back for breakfast.

"If it's not a further imposition," he said. "You must tell me if it is."

"We'll have ham and bagels," I said. "I brought bagels back from Montreal."

After he drove off, I realized that I had told them I'd been to Ottawa, not Montreal.

It didn't matter. It was late and nobody was thinking about

Canada any longer. Even the Russian was gone, somewhere over the ocean on a midnight flight. I stayed outside for a while, watching the tide come in. Inside the house, I got the impression Elena was moving through the rooms. Curious to see how I lived maybe. It didn't bother me. In fact, I was flattered. She came outside finally, and sat down in one of the rocking chairs.

"Did you like him?" she asked.

"Sure," I said. "He was very elegant. Do you think he's real?"

"Oh, what does it matter? Of course he's real. He's putting on a nice act. It suits him."

"Yes, it does."

"Did you see the loafers, the belt? Exquisite."

"Like a gigolo."

"Not that. A prince in hiding. Don't be petty, Jack. I wanted you to see him."

"I know you did. I wonder if he'll come back with the ham."

"Oh, I don't think so. But that doesn't change anything. We've got our memories." She smiled. A hard, clear smile. "I was thinking of working with him."

"What do you mean, working with him?"

"You know what I mean. I could use a partner. At least one."

All night, she hadn't mentioned anything about our trip to the water by Goose Neck. The crooked lawyer and the diamonds he was meant to be holding.

I had wondered whether she would mention it again. I'd been waiting for her to do it.

"You're not going to work with him," I said.

"Why not? He's got style. Elegance. You said it yourself. Might be just the thing I need."

"Go steal his car, if you're feeling restless."

"It was a beautiful car. I never wanted a car like that but then I saw his."

It sounded like she had thought about it. Maybe she had been thinking about it all evening, at La Vache, and elsewhere, ever since she laid eyes on him, whatever he was.

El Vizconde de Triacastela. It must have made her think of her father, hearing that ridiculous title. You could have asked her a dozen different ways, and she wouldn't have admitted it, but it must have occurred to her. A viscount from Spanish Galicia.

"What a story," she said. "Imagine taking it out, working with it."

"Didn't he say he was a psychiatrist? Maybe that part's true. He has insight."

"He didn't say it, not quite. He implied it. Very clever about the ambiguities."

"It was a good story. A double murder, Jesus."

"All those intricacies. The panache."

"I wonder who he tells it to. What's he looking for?"

"God, if I had a story like that, I'd tell it to everyone. I'd never stop working."

She was in a special mood. Feeling pleased after bringing around her discovery.

Back inside, she found another bottle of wine I had forgotten about. It was a dark Spanish red, and after she opened it, the bottle left a dark ring on the wood planks.

It would have to be worked out with sandpaper. Maybe the salt air would strip it away.

"Remind me why we never worked together," she said. "In the old days."

She was holding the glass beneath her chin, like a buttercup petal.

"A hundred reasons," I said.

"Remind me of a couple."

"You frighten me, to start. You confuse me too. Although I don't mind that so much."

She smiled. "Do you remember when we used to go on our holidays?"

"Breaking and entering."

"In the off-season. Who's hurt? We stole a few bottles of lousy wine. Some sardines."

"I remember. You'd pick the houses. And the locks. I'd scamper in behind you."

"You never scampered a day in your life. You enjoyed yourself. I thought you did."

"I did."

"So did I. But that was just playing around. Playing house. Snooping in cottages." She took a long sip of the wine. It looked almost black, lifted out of the light. "You're still wondering why I'm here," she said. "Why I've come back."

"Diamonds. You told me already. A job that demands doing. Aesthetic concerns."

"You're not taking me seriously. You think I'm just putting on a show."

"I don't know what to think. Honestly, Elena, I never do. I figured that's the point."

"You take me for a gigolo. Some Wellfleet psychiatrist."

"Not that, no. Neither of those."

"Some two-bit ham peddler. Taking a sob story out for a turn, seeing how it plays."

"He wasn't two-bit. You saw his car. That posture. He had grace."

"I'm glad you appreciated him. I wanted you to meet him. I'm really glad."

"But you're not going to partner up with him."

"Me? No. He was too perfect. Let him go his own way. He'll find an old lady to marry."

"Or a young one."

"I wouldn't mind having his car though. That was a great car. I wonder whose it is."

"Borrowed it from a friend. Maybe one of the psychiatrists."

For some reason, that made her laugh. I hadn't thought that it would, not really.

"Hell," she said, "we have fun, Jack, don't we? We've always kept each other guessing. That's why I've come. We're going to have some fun. I was sitting in my apartment in New York, alone, finally. Sitting around in these linen pajamas. I swear to you. You're meant to wash and dry them in the machine but you can't, they'll wrinkle and never be right again. I'm sitting in wrinkled pajamas and I realize—Jack needs me."

"For what exactly?"

"To save you."

I didn't ask her what from. It didn't matter.

She smiled again. I could hardly see her now in the dark. "You seem lonely, Jack."

"No, that's not it. Try something else."

"I mean it. I hadn't realized it until just now. Until now, I was only joking around."

She poured herself more wine, filling her glass then emptying half of it into mine.

It was a deft, needless movement, but impressive all the same. Something she had picked up during her waitressing days maybe, marrying the ketchups at the end of a night.

10

That week I got a call saying it was time to move the Stamford kid. There weren't too many arrangements to make. Some car rentals and a few maps to chart out. It had been a long time since I'd covered the Eastern Seaboard. They were going to move him out through Miami. Staying off toll roads, the round trip would take five days, maybe less. I told the kid to pack up, but he had never unpacked. It was a sad little cottage I'd put him in, and he hadn't tried to cheer it up any. There was no one for him to say goodbye to. He did all that months ago, cut ties, before he sold the information he'd stolen and put himself into the hands of people who held vague, lucrative grudges against one another—people who'd hired brokers and couriers and layer on layer of security teams and law firms. Anyway, the call came from Bruno and the kid was ready to go. I went to get him on Tuesday night. We were both sorry to miss pickup that week. We talked about it for a while. You needed something to talk about in those early, jagged moments and basketball was as good as anything else, and it calmed his nerves some. He told me about the college where he'd played, a technical college in Upstate New York. They ran a statistics-heavy system and shot a lot of threes, no offensive rebounds.

He seemed relieved to be on the move. It didn't matter where to. For most people it doesn't matter, not at first. Later on, they get stuck again and wish there had been a different starting point or that somebody had given them a push in another direction.

Staying off the highways helped. There was hardly any traffic and you got to see all those small towns and the people sitting around Walmart parking lots, doing nothing.

He asked if he could drive for a while. I said no, and it seemed to sting him.

We were in Pennsylvania then, near the Maryland border where the land gets lush.

I had called ahead and booked us two or three motels per night. Each motel was in a different town. Different names, rates, check-in times. Around seven I would start thinking about which one to go to. Chance would have been better, but you couldn't be sure of finding a place that would take you without a license or a credit card to hold the rooms.

We had a good meal outside Richmond, Virginia, and both rooms were clean. In the morning the owner of the motel came around with a wake-up call and coffee. He woke you up by tapping the mouth of a steel carafe against the window. He had big hopeful eyes and looked like he wanted you to stay an extra night on the house just to have someone to talk to. The next night we were at a Motel 6 in Georgia. The kid's room was full of watercolor paintings. Mine was empty, and I offered to switch when he told me about it, but he said it was fine, they weren't terrible paintings, only odd, and there were so many of them it made you feel like somebody was behind them, watching you.

There was always a lot of paranoia on the road. It was the safest place to be, if you planned it right. Still, there was exposure. A primitive part of your brain is always worried about the tall grass and snakes, and the horizon seems to shift every time you look at it. We got down to Florida and the kid went back to talking about basketball. He was remembering games he had played when he was in high school. Moments when he'd disappointed himself. The way his parents had looked at him one night when he walked off the court after an argument with the coach. He was the team's best player, and he walked off and forced them to finish the game without him. His parents were sitting there in the stands, watching it. Finally, his mother left the gym.

"Scottie Pippen did that once," I said.

The kid just shook his head. "It wasn't like that."

"What was it like?"

"That was Pippen's time and he wanted the ball. That's reasonable."

"What about you?"

"I didn't want anything. That was the point. I didn't want to owe anyone anything."

"A new name helps that kind of thing. If you're still feeling that way."

"That's interesting," he said. "I hadn't thought of that. Thanks."

He sounded like he wanted to believe it too.

I got a bad feeling once we were back on the coast. South Florida Atlantic is one long metropolitan border, with exits to the cities and the barrier islands on your left and the inland lakes on your right. In the summer heat, you could see lightning crackling over the swamps. Along the water were mangroves and clear skies, but the swamp was something different, and there was no forgetting what was there. We stopped for a meal at a Denny's in Fort Lauderdale. I wasn't sorry to see the kid go, only I didn't want to get to the drop too early. We'd made better time than I expected through Palm Beach. There should have been traffic for hours, but it was like we were the only car on the road for a stretch of ten, fifteen miles. We both ordered French toast. I'd never seen anyone use so much syrup as the kid used. It was right up to the lip of his plate. The waitress called him sweetheart, and after I paid the check he left a hundred-dollar bill on the table, in a saucer. It was his money. I didn't ask about it.

The drop was at Rickenbacker Marina, 9:00 p.m. We were twenty minutes early.

"Are they taking me to Cuba?" he asked. He sounded excited, like he was on vacation.

"Maybe," I said. "Probably Bimini from here. If it were Cuba, we'd be in the Keys."

"Bimini? That's the Bahamas."

"They'll take you to Nassau from there. From Nassau, it's up to you."

It was more than I should have told him. More than I knew. I was just guessing.

He was looking out at the water. Across the bay was the city, overgrown and lurid.

"I wouldn't stay in Nassau," I said. "You'll have papers if you want to travel."

"Why wouldn't you stay?"

"It's cloistered and for sale. Don't stay in any of the big island towns. All the lawyers spend afternoons at the yacht clubs, bartering. They'll trade you in if they get a chance."

"Trade me for what?"

The question hung there for a minute, and we got out of the car.

There were two men getting the boat ready. The small mean-looking one took the kid's bag and put it in the hold while the other man made small talk, asking about the drive, where we had been, had we seen anything, what did we think of Miami, not bad, huh? I'd met him before but couldn't remember where. He had a faint accent. Dutch maybe.

"I worked with your father once," he said to me. "Long time ago. He's good?"

"He's fine, thanks."

"He likes it up there, huh? Doesn't want to retire, come down here like everyone else?"

"No, he likes it there."

"He's got a woman," the man said. It wasn't a question, but a certainty. A truism.

Every people-smuggler is a philosopher in his own squalid way, the same as spies.

The moment was dragging on longer than it needed to, and I realized I'd lost track of the smaller man after he went into the hold. He might have been down there still, or in the marina office arranging things for their return or calling ahead to Bimini, but I didn't think so. I looked around and didn't see him anywhere. It was a dark, quiet place, that marina, no different than a thousand others except I'd brought the kid there.

The small man came from behind and wrapped a cord around the kid's neck. When it broke through skin, there was a rush of blood, then a hollow pop as the windpipe collapsed. The kid had his hands up but couldn't find a grip. His legs gave out beneath.

"Jesus," the big man said. "Be quick about it, okay? Don't fuck around this time."

The small man twisted the cord and twisted it again and the kid's throat seemed to wither down to a stalk, and the weight of his head was too much. His tongue was out.

It lasted maybe a minute, no more than two. There was no fight and hardly any noise.

When it was done, the big man helped carry him onto the boat. "Be right back," he said.

They came back and shared a rag between them, cleaning their hands.

"That's finished," the big man said. "Nasty business. He seemed a fine young man."

The small man said something in their language. I didn't think it was Dutch anymore.

"He says we have to go," the big man told me. "The tide is the issue. Always the tide."

The small man nodded. His hands, wiped clean with the rag, were folded together. They seemed quite soft to me but couldn't have been. It must have been the blood pumping there after the work with the cord that gave them the look of being delicate.

Neither of them offered an explanation. Maybe they thought I'd been read-in already.

There wasn't any traffic on the causeway, or in the city either. I decided to drive through the night. Around Fort Lauderdale, my hands began shaking. Like an earthquake registering a day later, somewhere out in the ocean, stirring up the waves.

PART II

11

waited a couple of days after getting home. I didn't want to see anyone. It was better not to see anyone, coming off a thing like that. You needed to walk awhile first. Not a jog or a trot or any other kind of exercise but a slow, steady walk. I circled the harbor a few times and went around to check on clients. I stopped only to speak with one. The rest I merely looked in on. I stopped at a few innocent houses too. The paranoia stays with you for a time, and it always feels like you've picked up a tail, so you knock on a few doors and ask if they've heard the good news. Make conversation for a minute in case anyone's watching. If there's a family inside, move on. Try not to involve anyone. You're a man without cares, just bored or looking to be neighborly. The static is the point. There's something following you and the static is the one good way to be rid of it.

I kept thinking about the men from the boat and the rag they cleaned their hands with.

And how the kid had asked whether he could drive, and I hadn't let him.

How nobody had bothered to read me in. I was only the ferryman, come to shore.

It kept up like that for two days and change, then I went to see Elena. It was early in the day, and she was working at the kitchen table, surrounded by papers and chewing on the end of a pen. I watched her through the open window for a moment and contemplated the various reasons why I had come. She looked so lost in her work I almost turned around, but then she saw me. "Come inside," she said. "There's coffee."

She was staying in a cottage on Huckleberry Street. Her family, what was left of it, didn't know she was there. Most of them lived on Winthrop Point, a peninsula across the harbor channel where there were a few old houses and a seminary. You used to see the seminarians across the water. They came onto the beach in the morning to do their absolutions. Sometimes they would feed the deer. The deer were there to lick salt off the rocks when the tide was out and to get what they could from the monks. A quiet section of town, and removed. Elena had decided to rent a cottage near the village center. It wasn't an extravagant place, but it was on the higher end for Onset. Two thousand a month in summer. It was owned by a family in North Adams. They came only for a week in May, then rented it out for the season. She was using the living room and kitchen as an office.

I made it through the first cup. We both did. Then I asked if she was serious about it.

"Serious about what?"

"Goose Neck. Paulson, with the diamonds."

She frowned. "Very serious. Jack, you don't know what it's been like these last years."

She closed her computer and unplugged some electronics lying around the kitchen. Leave it to a lawyer to be more careful than anyone. She signaled for me to follow, and we went outside. The yard was kelly green, a loud, unnatural color so close to salt water. The gardener was there working on some roses. He was Hungarian but went by the name Sullivan. He helped to maintain a lot of properties on the shore. He waved hello.

"He's glad to see I've got a friend," she said. "He worries about me."

We walked down to the beach toward the harbor. Our shoes were back on the lawn.

Without my asking her to, she explained what she was planning. It seemed to me she was vain about the details. It had all been carefully worked out and justified. Frank Paulson, a senior partner at her firm, a summer resident of Goose Neck, was holding rough diamonds valued at either three million dollars or one hundred and eighty million dollars, depending on whether you were addressing the tax authorities of the exporting or importing nation. The discrepancy was part of a laundry. The stones needed to live somewhere discreet for a month, then would ship out on a journey through Panama to Russia, en route to Europe. Paulson was proud of the trust his clients had in him, the crooks in particular. He was an old New England Brahmin. They had all sorts of fetishes and strange dispositions. He was keeping the stones in a wall safe, with light security put in place by the insurers, who were not insurers in any traditional sense, because the diamonds were not really diamonds but currency in gray-market transactions. Everything was off books, she told me, until it was time to pay out.

"Have you got access to the safe?" I asked.

She shook her head. Her arm was looped through mine, very casually.

"Somebody on the inside, his wife maybe?"

"God, no. They sleep in separate bedrooms. It's one of those marriages."

"Then you're the one inside. You're working the laundry with him."

"He keeps me away from the dirtiest stuff. Like a daughter."

We talked it over for a while, very matter-of-factly, calmly. Her arm felt cool against my side. It was a great deal of money, if you could move the diamonds after. But you had to know what kind of people used rough diamonds in their day-to-day financial transactions. The kind who had money, also, to hire Paulson, a lawyer who billed over a thousand dollars for an hour of his time like every other self-respecting extortionist attorney did just then. The diamonds were from Angola, she said, and headed for Antwerp. A dozen stops in between. That was the point: creating a trail that would tie you in knots. During any one of those stops, they might be swapped out for fakes and moved along. In Antwerp they would know, or would soon figure it out, but not before.

"The risk is built in," she said. "They'll write it down. Shrinkage, same as Walmart."

"If you can get them out of the safe."

"Don't tease me, Jack, it isn't fair. If you came here to talk me out of it, you can leave."

"I haven't come to talk you out of it."

"Of course you have. You're the voice of reason. The conscience I never asked for."

"What happens to Paulson after?"

"Nothing. It's so goddamn tidy, Jack. He collects his fees, carries on with his life."

"Until the diamonds hit Antwerp."

"Passing through how many hands on the way? Grubby, sweaty hands, any of which could have boosted them. They know it. I'm telling you, it's built in. It'll never land back on Paulson. As long as it's done cleverly, he won't feel it. He won't ever need to."

I could hear that it was a conversation she had already conducted with herself. There was a moral undergirding to it. An imperative that had nearly formed.

I told her I wanted in, if she would have me. Lawyer, monk, smuggler, spy—it all sounded the same just then. I thought, Why not add thief to the list? I wanted to take something that didn't belong to me. I wanted money and never to work another job I didn't understand. Stealing was clean, almost immaculate, and it opened up other possibilities and futures. I didn't say any of that. I asked her if she had a team. I asked how far along the planning was and what my cut would be. All the questions I presumed you were meant to ask of collaborators in a situation like that one.

For the first time in days, or maybe much longer than that, I felt good and almost loose.

"I'll show you everything I've got," she said. "Christ, we're going to have some fun."

She sounded genuine about it. Like she had missed me, as I had her.

There, on the beach, quite ceremoniously, we shook hands. She went back to her cottage, and I went to the office and looked through casework I'd been neglecting. I hadn't been in the office for a while and the names of all those clients who were coming into town and those who were scheduled to leave seemed to me a great, undefinable burden.

It was Friday. I had missed another pickup game the night before. You started to feel it in your muscles when you missed too many games. Other kinds of exercise weren't enough. You wanted to get out and run, and if you went straight to it you might do something wild, but if you sat with the restlessness for a time it would settle, like a drug.

12

Frank Paulson came from old Cape stock. His family had been around before the canal and owned some of the land and riparian rights that had been used to dig it. When the enterprise proved less profitable than investors had hoped, a group of them put word in the Boston papers that German ships and spies had been seen skulking around Cape Cod Bay, troubling the shipping lanes. Soon afterward, the government agreed to take the whole misbegotten adventure off their hands, at retail. A respectable piece of business undertaken by the old families, the ones who were around even earlier than the Spiritualists. They had Puritan blood running through their veins. It made them hard and quick to judge. They threw regattas and masquerades at summer's end.

I didn't know any other way to come at him, so I gave him a rundown, like I would for anyone else.

His legal practice was impeccable. The firm billed him at

$1,050 an hour. His name was all over the public record, signed at the ends of briefs and delivering keynotes at professional gatherings and the occasional charity fundraiser. He had real estate holdings in New York and New England and pieces of four or five trust funds.

It was due diligence. Background work. Names, paper trails, bank accounts. But I was hoping, also, to find something. I wanted to bring it to her. Or I wanted to see it for myself. I kept at it for a few days and thought about what it would take to make him pull the diamonds himself. Take them for a ride somewhere. Maybe have them appraised, if he thought that they were fugazi—that he was being set up by someone in the laundry chain, left holding a bag. That was the easiest, cleanest way. Elena knew it too.

She didn't think he would take them out himself, no matter the pressure applied, however you tried to bind him.

She had it all worked out, the ideas and plans. I figured there was no harm in bringing her something more. It felt like that moment in a pickup game when the action starts and you're still feeling out your team. Taking things slowly and learning who you'll be.

"He never goes anywhere," she said. "The mountains all come rushing to him."

And even if he bit, there were the security guards. They weren't his employees but more like colleagues or watchers. It was all billed out to the clients. The clients were some Bariloche Argentines with German names whose business had been at the firm since the family washed up in the Americas after World War II, with a cardinal's backing, Swiss nationality, and mining interests that extended to the days of parchment.

Through gray-market insurers and other intermediaries, the Argentines were ultimately paying for the guards. But for only two of them. Doing it on the cheap probably appealed to Paulson. Maybe he had convinced them two was all it took. Money was always a little backward in New England; the old families never wanted to spend any of it. That was how they had stuck around so long, feeding off the interest, pinching their pennies.

The security could be beat, was my feeling. Any setup can, if you stare at it long enough. Theirs was more than you might expect to find in a summer home but pretty paltry all the same. Two men and a wall safe. The natural isolation of the land, the unlikelihood of it all.

Shooting off the flare had been a wild, maybe even reckless move, but it gave us a clear look at the guards, and she wasn't wrong to want it. You could tell things from that: The way they worked together or didn't. The way they positioned themselves. Things beyond the apparent and having nothing to do with if they were armed or carrying radios or cameras, or following in a formation, nor whether they were high end, military.

Those were good and useful things to know, but it was also important just to see them.

Something told me one of them had his foot out, or that he was straddling some other line. It was nothing specific, nothing I could have put into words. Just the way he went bounding down the stone stairs toward the dock after lingering at the top, considering his options. Wondering what it was worth.

So I looked him up. Gave him the same rundown, layer by layer.

His name was Kalianidis. No military background. He used to work the gatehouse at the Fore River Shipyard in Braintree. He took some night classes. He was thirty-two, with a few debts still hanging around from his three semesters at UMass Boston. Nothing too heavy, no bad habits, a few friends. His father ran a pizza shop in Brockton.

I wanted to see him again and parked myself on the only road in or out. I figured he would show up at some point and I would see him and then there would be more to it.

I had followed people before, many times, more than I could count or remember. It was part of the tradecraft, and it could be done well with a team leapfrogging or working with a grid, but you could manage almost as well alone if you were subtle about it and quiet and didn't mind losing your target here and there, trusting that you would pick him up again. Which you would, if you knew the terrain at least as well as or, ideally, better than the person you were trailing.

Kalianidis drove out in the Paulsons' Escalade. He covered the mile into the village center, then doubled back. It wasn't an evasive measure. He was lost, so he stopped at a gas station and asked, awkwardly, for directions. Trying to look very professional about it. Like he was going to draw a map.

People used to ask what it was like growing up with a spy for a father. I would tell them different things that amounted to nothing or it would become a joke. I would tell them about the two-way he'd rigged in my bedroom when I was young, just after my mother left, and how at night he would talk to me through it and say that it was God talking, and I should behave well at school and wash between my toes and not pay my father too much deference because adults had to earn it just like anyone else. It went on for four or five nights, then he quit and took out the bug and later on told me that it had made him nervous, the way I accepted the situation so matter-of-factly and hadn't told anyone what was happening but kept my own counsel instead. Small things like that, which had happened and could be told like a story you would bring to parties and second dates. And about the goofy little things he did—threads across the doorjambs, rocks on tires. Always catching me when I would sneak out. The truth was, it was like any relationship, only more acute. It sometimes felt like he could read my every thought.

Elena was the only person who never asked me what it was like. Who never even hinted at it. I got the impression she knew already. Another thing she had pieced together without having to be told. Or she had me marked from the day we met in Jacobs Neck.

13

decided to visit my father. I hadn't seen him since the Florida run. He was out on the lawn, looking toward the water, slumped down in an Adirondack chair, telling himself
stories. When he smoked alone, he sometimes recounted old
operations to himself. He changed details to prove that he
could. A mental exercise. Besides the hash and other hobbies
he'd picked up over the years, he had a lot of exercises and
truly believed in some of them, though he wouldn't tell you
which ones.

That night he was telling himself a story about an operation in Tripoli. Not the city in Libya but in Lebanon. It had
to do with a man who owned a sweets factory. I had heard a
version of the story before. I came up the path through the
garden and sat down beside him. It was a ridiculous thing for
an old spy to be doing. That was the appeal. He had a Shake-
spearean side that you didn't always sense from a distance. At

school he was in plays. My mother told me that once. Musicals and tragedies, she said, nothing in between.

"Catch that game last night?" he asked.

"Sure," I said. "Didn't think they'd get it in before the rain."

"Always looks that way, doesn't it? Then, a break in the clouds."

There wasn't any game the night before. He was playing around, talking in the old codes. He would sit around stoned, murmuring stories about Lebanon for anyone to hear, but when his son shows up that's what he asks about: a phantom Red Sox game.

He had been living alone for too long. Caterina, his friend, had a place of her own on North Smith Street. She was going to inherit a triple-decker in Brockton, too, and then rent out all three floors and quit teaching but carry on coaching field hockey and visiting my father. She was a strong-willed woman. She wouldn't have married him if he'd asked, and he had never asked, so far as I was aware.

"Want to keep going on that story?" I asked. "Tripoli. Factory man. He makes, what, kanafeh?"

He shook his head. "Baklava. He's pretending to be Greek. That's why I need him."

The detail sounded familiar. Baklava. Had he pulled it from somewhere? A novel? He liked Graham Greene but never the spy novels. He liked the morality plays and whiskey priests. Maybe there really was baklava involved. He had a taste for desserts.

"Have you spoken with Bruno?" I asked.

He nodded. "Called in, when, a week ago? You were on the road. I looked in on the wires. You know Bruno, he doesn't explain because he can't. He would like to. He's got a song in his heart but doesn't know the lyric, doesn't know the melody. He's part of that generation of Italian men, reared on silent milk farms in Bensonhurst. But he's sorry. He fucked it up. Tried getting you word, but then you were already on the move."

"I checked in."

"Maybe he didn't try too hard. They expect you to be stoic. Maybe he was testing you. The point is this: it wasn't your fault, what went on down there. These things happen. Blood sacrifices, call them. Down through the ages, it gets spilled. It has to sometimes."

"That's bullshit."

He shrugged. He was slumped down in that Adirondack. In the dying light, I could hardly see him, and the obscurity gave him a playful air. Or it was the smoke that did it.

"Did you try walking it off?" he asked. "Walking helps."

"Yes."

"But you've been up to other things this week. More than walking."

He was smiling faintly. Nodding to himself, or just fighting back the tremors.

We were coming around to it now. You could feel it approaching, like a wave.

"A little pastime," he said, "a hobby, say, can be useful. Keeps the mind sharp and sensitive to new intakes, keeps you pliable. Otherwise, tunnel vision, operation fever, none of it good, right? But what am I trying to tell you, Jack? Don't you know already?"

I wasn't going to answer his questions for him. Not the ones he didn't bother to ask.

"You're enjoying spending time with her," he said. "That's all right too. It's summer. But you've got to remember your line. She's got one line of work, and you can dress it up however you like, but it's her line, and she's good at it and can thrive there. You're something else. That can be a powerful attraction, but it's just that, and you've got to be careful. Careful with your time, your heart. All of it. People will use you up."

He took a long drag off his pipe. The smoke smelled sweet. A honeysuckle note.

"We're supposed to be the ones using them," I said. "That's what you mean."

"If you like."

"I don't much, is the point."

"Ah," he said, nodding again. "So that's the point."

There was more I wanted to say. I had seen people dead and dying but never delivered one to it before. It was different than seeing it happen. Different than cleaning up after it. Cleaning up after a client chose an end was part of the job. You began to understand the ways it was and could be done. That was an education in men, women, and their sorrowful inventions. Delivering them to it was different. Handing them over like a gift.

We were quiet for a while and then he told me something more about Tripoli.

"I needed him to burn up a boat," he said. "The man with the factory. A boat full of sweets that he'd bought out from a rival. Took over the man's business, ran him into ruin, and commandeered the inventory. He was shipping it over. But the ship was out of Cyprus and it was useful for us to have it burn; a claim made on the insurance. We were smoking someone out, you could say. This man, he worked half his life to take over the other's business. But we needed him to burn it. Know how I convinced him? I told him to do it on a whim, because he could. Throw a match to it all."

"I thought the ship was from Greece."

"The Greek side of Cyprus. Are you following me, Jack? This might be important."

"Or it might be bullshit."

"That's right. It's for you to decide. Are you feeling any better? I'm trying here, son."

He didn't call me son. I didn't call him Dad. It might as well have been another code. This was how he cheered you. How he bucked you up for more. Every man, a handler.

"I'm fine," I said. "Don't worry about me. You were right. The walking helped."

"Ambulatory care. Talking's not bad either. Except for the Italians—they want to sing."

I used to think about him sometimes. My father in the Middle East, North Africa. Younger than I was then. He had gone into the service because his draft number came in low. They would have sent him as infantry to Vietnam like they had his brothers, except he tested an aptitude for languages, so they trained him in signals and Russian at the Naval Language Institute in Monterey, a cliff-top monastery filled with spies and dissidents. Then they sent him to Cyprus and turned him loose. A strange way for a young man to meet the world, but he made it through his term and signed up for more.

When he first got back to the States, he walked in his sleep. He jumped out a second-floor window once, thinking there was Agent Orange seeping through the walls. He thought that he had been dosed with LSD, or that my mother or I had been. This was when I was a baby. The first clients he took on were from a radical cell in Cambridge. They put a bomb in a police station and called in a warning. Nobody was hurt but there had been enough bombings by then. The FBI was brought in, so the radicals needed to leave. Two he took to Canada. Another one was determined to settle in Idaho. It was easy enough to arrange back then. He had contacts from the service and the agencies. They were mostly back stateside and maybe some of them were having those same dreams. Slowly, he built up a network. From the radical cells, you were soon working with traffickers and gunrunners, then the mobs. He didn't draw too many distinctions. All of them criminals. Spies were different, he told me once, like the clergy.

He believed that sort of thing. You had to love a man who could lie to himself that way.

Lying to yourself was at the heart of the matter. You had to do it with a kind of joy.

"Ever think about practicing?" he asked.

"Practicing what?"

I knew what he meant but the question caught me off guard.

"Country lawyer always seemed to me a decent life," he said. "A proper legal practice."

"I don't mind the work. That's not what this is about."

"I didn't say you did. Only you have options—know that. Not everyone does."

"They'd disbar me within a year if I tried practicing."

"You don't believe that, do you? I'd put money on you making it three years at least. Maybe you should take in a few cases anyway. Just something for the cover. Anyone ever comes looking, it might seem odd if you didn't have a few things on the docket, don't you think? Then who knows, you might like it. You might find it suits your temperament. A person's temperament changes over the course of his life, like a river."

I could barely see him, but I could feel him smiling. Waiting for me to rise to the bait.

"Sure," I said. "I've always wanted to try wingtips. Maybe hire a paralegal."

"Think about it. You'd never have to go to Florida again. Not until you retire."

"Fuck off."

"What, you don't want to retire? A nice little two bedroom in East Boca. No, that's not for us, is it, Jack? For you and me, we've got our place, our town, and it's right here. Our East Boca of the midnight soul. What would happen to all this if we weren't here?"

There, he had finally come around to it. It was as close as he would get to saying it.

"Think about it, Jack. It's always worth thinking about."

There were scallops inside, and he asked me to cook them. Flash fried, on the pan.

After dinner, he was feeling better and got dessert out of the fridge. A key lime pie.

"Made it myself," he said. "The secret is using all those fucking limes."

I didn't want to laugh but found myself headed that way and finally gave over to it.

"You didn't make this," I said.

"Sure I did. The restorative power of acid and cream, you can't beat it."

"Go to hell."

"I wouldn't know which way to turn. Just eat your pie, huh? That's your dad's pie."

He fell asleep beside me in his chair. I had to wake him to go in for the night.

14

It was around four. Elena and I were at the Sam'l Allen Inn in Sandwich. They were very particular about the apostrophe and how it was pronounced. It was among the oldest continuously operating establishments on the Cape. In the lobby was an air of semi-ancient grandeur that had never quite been realized, except in the imaginations of certain wedding guests, local gentry, and long-standing midlevel employees. The bartender was a man called Rudolfo. Trim, athletic, pale, plainspoken. Rounding forty.

Few people had ever struck me as less likely to be called Rudolfo but that's what he went by, and it was how I introduced him to Elena. I had paid him earlier and a few times before that in the past, for odds and ends, the kinds of things a clever, steady hand in the hospitality industry could be called on to provide. Now he was ready to chat. Looking pleased to see us and solicitous. He hid his cleverness under the livery.

I always liked the way he conducted himself behind the bar. He kept glasses polished and orderly but appeared as though he were doing it for himself, like he would have kept them that way whether or not he had customers. The rest of the inn was worn at the seams. I had always been led to believe there was a tearoom somewhere that was understated and elegant. Elena asked for a tonic water with lots of ice and a lime twist.

"So what is there to learn here?" she asked. "Or is this just a change of scenery?"

Rudolfo looked to me.

"Tell her," I said.

He leaned his elbows on the bar. His eyes had an odd crystalline quality to them.

"They're coming in," he said. "Dependably, like they're on patrol. They arrive in the same car, hers I figure, although he drives and opens the door for her and walks into the hotel first. Playing the security man, which is what I'm told he is. Checks the lobby for something, I don't know what. Suspicious characters. Makes a little show of it, then signs them into room 208. They like that one, room 208. I guess they call ahead to reserve it, because they always seem to get right in."

She had her chin in her hand, smiling, keeping her attention fixed until he was done.

Then, turning to me, she asked who it was we were talking about, exactly. Still smiling.

"Kalianidis," I said. "The security guard living at Paulson's."

"Having himself a summer fling. But with whom?"

"Paulson's wife."

Now, finally, a break in her repose. "Billie?"

"I have her name down as Willa. Is that not what she goes by?"

"Billie Paulson. Christ, Jack. You are industrious. What else? There's more."

I let Rudolfo tell her when it started.

"One month ago," he said. "They haven't missed a date yet."

"How often do they come in?"

"One good roll a week. They book room 208, Tuesday nights. They show up between four and four thirty in the afternoon when the place is empty. They go upstairs. Twenty to twenty-five minutes later, they order champagne. Sometimes they drink it, sometimes it warms the ice and I use it for Bellinis the next day. Dinner, same thing: up to the room. They order around eight. Sometimes after dinner, when it's dark, they take a walk around the lawn. The guy, he plays at being a security man again, walks ahead of her a step. Looks around. Asks the staff questions nobody needs answered. Then they go back to the room and have a little more exercise. They leave between ten thirty and eleven the same night and the staff uses the room to throw dice."

I could see now that she was enjoying herself. Enjoying Rudolfo and seeing his cleverness and the way he kept the bar. She was glad I had brought her. I could have told her about it, but this was better—bringing her—and that was what I owed her. What we owed each other. Or maybe it was just the worn, fading opulence of the surroundings. Elena ordered another drink. We both did, and Rudolfo brought them over.

"I'll leave you two to discuss it," he said.

What did he think we were up to? He was enjoying him-

self, too, with money in his pocket. Then the doors opened
and a bridal party came in and he saw the rest of his afternoon
unfolding, for good or ill, and he left us in earnest. He had a
living to make.

"So they're down a security guard once a week," she said
when we were alone. "Are we sure they don't bring in a re-
placement that night? That they break rank like that?"

"They're too cheap for anything else. That old Cape par-
simony."

"You've been watching them. How often?"

"Every chance I get."

"Without anyone noticing, I hope."

"I hope so, yes."

"Otherwise you wouldn't be very good at your day job.
This is lovely, Jack. Really."

"I'm glad you think so."

"And what do you think? Will it last?"

"The affair? I don't know. It's what you said—a fling, I
presume."

She thought about it for a while. Sucking on an ice cube
pulled from her drink.

"No," she said. "It'll last. It's her first. Forty years married;
she's been honest. So it's more than a fling. It means everything to her. She's religious about it. Spends all day getting herself ready, laying out her clothes. Won't let him see her before,
like a bride."

Her eyes narrowed like she was watching it play out in
front of us. Trying to focus.

"Paulson could find them out," I said. "That would end it."

"Not a chance," she said. "His world is self-regarding. His wife is his reflection."

"Okay, so we've got, conservatively, a five-hour window when there's one security guard in the house instead of two. But we've still got the one to deal with. Not to mention Paulson, unless you know when he's leaving the house. Plus, domestic staff."

"How many do you think?"

"Staff? I don't know. Cape people are funny about that. Day workers probably."

"I mean, how many for the job? What's your count? I know you're keeping a tally. You're impossibly practical. It's one of the things I love about you, Jack. I can see that little ticker tape rolling out of your ears. Logistics."

We talked through various numbers and possibilities. Or rather, I did. As I droned on the room began to darken. Outside, the sun had fallen below the tree line. Another man in livery that didn't quite match the one Rudolfo and the waiters were wearing came into the bar with a long-handled torch, looking like he was going to use it to light chandeliers and other items overhead. He carried it out in front of him, balanced against his hip bone, walked twice around the room, a kind of parade. Then, when the bridal party had had enough of his charms, he discreetly flipped an electric switch and filled the room with a warm glow. An old-fashioned glow, from another time, like the rest of it.

"It's sweet that this is where she wants to come," Elena said. "Her first affair and she knew just where she wanted to have it. It's not out of the way either. Somebody will see her here, but you can tell she just had to have it here or it wouldn't have felt the same. People are so obstinate about their dreams. And she has him order the champagne too."

"And open doors for her."

"Carries her over the threshold. But who pays for it?"

"A credit card in her maiden name. An old account. Nothing joint."

She went quiet for a time, maybe thinking about bank statements and maiden names.

Then she smiled. The smile one reserves for memories. "Just you and me," she said. "Two."

"Two what?" I asked.

"Two people in our team. Getting the job done right, that's all it should take."

"Two people," I said, with doubt in my voice.

"Well," she said. "Two people with full knowledge."

"Full knowledge?"

"Others in support, walled off."

"Like Rudolfo."

"Performing discrete tasks."

"Am I going to meet the others? Or do you want to go on with flattery and lies?"

"I wouldn't flatter you, Jack. Never. You're in my confidence. I'm in yours."

"So what happens when our one security guard is at the Sam'l Allen Inn making passionate tightly secured love to the esteemed Mrs. Paulson and the other, his colleague, is sitting at home next to the safe making sure his one-man protection holds?"

"That's true. It would be better to have some misdirection in place, don't you think?"

"Which takes manpower."

"But not ours necessarily."

"Got anything particular in mind?"

"Of course I do. We're on a clock here, aren't we? Summer won't last forever."

"So we're talking a rush job. Two people. Flash, smash, and grab. Get caught. Lunacy."

"Don't talk like that, Jack. You sound like a fool."

"All right."

"Come on, let's go. Tomorrow I'm going to show you my diamonds."

I didn't ask what she meant. It all seemed so impossible and immediate.

15

In the morning, after a big breakfast, we drove to Tremont Pond, where the Hasids had a camp in the woods. Starting in June, they came on buses from Williamsburg, Bed-Stuy, and the old industrial towns in the Hudson Valley. They'd been coming since the sixties. You never saw them on the beach, but you would see them walking the bluffs Saturday nights, sometimes in pairs on dates, and then a van would return them home.

She had arranged with Benjamin Navordny to make replica stones. Imitation rough diamonds. Navordny was a nonbeliever who had been coming to the Tremont camp since he was a kid. He was no longer part of the spiritual community, but he liked the season, its rhythms, and went to his family's cabin most weekends throughout July and August.

Elena had stayed in touch with him over the years. He had a shop on Forty-Seventh Street and ran an after-hours out of a Williamsburg warehouse. He was a wholesaler and a fence, among other pursuits. I had dealt with him many times. There were always clients looking to barter. Sometimes they carried stones in the lining of their jackets or suitcases. Things they had taken or held on to for rainy days and exits. I found Navordny to be professional when it came to the gems he was dealing, although often he was stoned. The weed was part of his loss of faith. He would tell anybody about it. How he'd had the faith and then lost it.

Evidently he was a forger too. Elena's forger, working for a flat fee. That wasn't something I had ever asked or needed him for, but it didn't surprise me.

When we got to the camp, Navordny was sitting on the front porch of his cabin smoking a blunt and keeping a narrow eye on a group of elders passing him by. It was Shabbat. There was a hush around camp, except for the crickets, which lived in the pines.

Navordny was wearing modern clothes. Jeans and a crisp white button-down. His shirt sleeves were rolled and his forearms tattooed. I wondered why the elders let him stick around but had never asked anyone about it. It was possible he did work for them, or knew their secrets, or else they were just hoping that he would come back into the fold.

"It was very good of you to come all this way," he said, still on the porch. He hadn't moved from his rocking chair. It was difficult to know whether he was being serious or using an empty show of manners to accentuate some point he was making. To us, or maybe to the old men walking by. He stood up and kissed Elena's cheek. He wore cologne. Something light, floral, almost feminine. On his arm, the tattoos were flowers.

"And you, Mr. Betancourt," he said. He held out his hand for me to shake. Holding it stiff, cupped, and turned over, like he was trying to keep something liquid in his palm.

"Hello, Benjamin."

"Are you here on behalf of a client? Or escorting our friend?"

"He's here with me," Elena said.

"That's interesting to learn," he said. "But then, two lawyers, why shouldn't you associate? Makes perfect sense, of course. Forgive me for asking. I was only surprised."

He watched me a moment, then looked at the hand I had shaken. Studied it.

The way he had said the word *lawyers* made it sound like a very old, poignant joke.

I liked him, despite myself. For some reason we had always done our business outdoors. En plein air, he would say when suggesting a place. He would take a vigorous drag of the salt air through his nose, and you couldn't help but do the same.

"How is your work?" Elena asked, taking his arm now. "Not an easy job I gave you."

"Easy, no," he said. "Enjoyable though. It's more like art. Polishing, any cretin can do."

"Nothing like that for you, Benjamin."

"You're kind. Come in. See what you've bought."

The inside of the cabin was decorated in the style of midcentury suburbia, with wallpaper and velour furniture in muted reds and greens. There were some family portraits on the walls and a record player in the corner. It was playing a Paul Simon album, of all things. You got the feeling there was somebody else there in the cabin, somebody other than Benjamin, but there were only two rooms and the doors were open and his parents had long since died. One room served as his office. That was where he showed us the stones he'd made. His forgeries. It was the kind of job you wouldn't give to just anyone in the Diamond District, even among the backroom dealers. Benjamin was an artist, in the end. It took a lot of inspiration to leave the community the way he had, without really leaving it, or without allowing it to leave him. He put the stones on satin and lit them up for us to inspect. Elena took the loupe.

"They're gorgeous," she said after not speaking for a while.

"Not everyone can appreciate a rough diamond," Benjamin said. "The rudimentary intimidates them. They think it looks like just another rock, or the color is too subtle."

He poured coffee and had more to say on the subject. There were a great many things your average person was not equipped to appreciate about rough diamonds. He had put a lot of effort into simulating them, and the result, in his estimation, was sublime.

"As though yesterday pulled from Mother Africa," he said. He sounded very serious.

There were seven stones varying dramatically in shape and hew, though all had a slightly green maritime tint. I looked at them under the lights for a while in case a moment came around later when I had to pretend to know something true about them.

"I know better than to ask what they're for," Benjamin said.

Elena smiled. She was having a second coffee. The coffee was thin, hardly more than water.

"The insurers want them," she said. "Client can't transport without a set of duplicates."

"Insurers are always asking for things. They don't know how to take a bet."

"All the same, I'd appreciate discretion."

He stepped back, momentarily insulted. It was another simulation. There was nothing but discretion in his line of work. An ancient line, derived from the mysterious and the unknown.

They chatted for a while over the thin coffee while I continued looking at the stones. They were talking about people and places I didn't know. A lot of names and offices.

It seemed they had known each other fairly well in New York, but I didn't ask for specifics and neither of them offered any. Elena had a life there that I knew almost nothing about.

After we were done with the inspection, Benjamin asked us to walk with him by the pond.

"There's a little pathway," he said. "It goes by everyone's door. We watch one another."

I hadn't spent much time around the camp. The pond was small, maybe a quarter-mile wide and a little more than that in length. The inlands were pocked with kettle ponds, left behind by retreating glaciers and connected now by the old tracts of pine and cranberry bog. Not many of those tracts were settled, but the ones that were had grown up like mountain valleys with their own communities and cultures; and when there were outsiders among them walking along the pond's shores, everybody knew, or seemed to. Benjamin was enjoying himself. He took Elena's hand for a stretch. It was midday and there was no shade along the pond's edge. There were two spots where beach sand had been poured but nobody was swimming. The pond water was very still.

Benjamin whistled. It was one of the Paul Simon songs, the almost African ones.

"Let them stare," he said. He was talking about his neighbors, inside, out of the sun.

He was in an enviable mood. Resplendent almost. In any case, altogether high.

He put an arm over my shoulder. "You'll help me, won't you, Mr. Betancourt?"

"Help you with what?" I asked.

"When they come for me. You'll help me, won't you? I could use a friend."

He was smiling and looking off into the distance, past the cottages, into the woods.

"Sure," I said. "You know where to find me, Benjamin."

"I appreciate that you don't ask me who will come," he said. Then, turning to Elena: "Our friend knows, it could be anyone. History teaches us this."

"Oh no," she said. "He's done with all that. He's with me now, don't you remember?"

"Yes," he said. "I remember: two lawyers. Still, all the world's a fucking Cossack."

She patted his hand. A tender moment. He muttered something too low to hear.

After we were done parading, Benjamin went back to his rocking chair, unbuttoned his shirt down to the belt, and opened it so that the sun would hit his chest. There were children playing next to his porch. Five of them with Hula-Hoops.

I was driving and Elena was in the passenger seat. She put the diamonds into the glove compartment, then changed her mind and held on to them with her left hand. They were in a satin bag. The inside of the car was very hot though we'd parked in the shade.

"I feel sorry for him," she said. "Alone out there."

"He seems content," I said.

"You can't really think that—he's miserable. But at least he has his work."

"How much did you pay for them?"

"Five thousand. How does that strike you?"

"I wouldn't know. Would you?"

She shrugged. "I trust Benjamin. Anyway, it's all just an expense. Another write-off."

With her finger, she wrote something in the air. An expense report or a tax filing maybe.

16

decided to meet with Tommy alone. It was Thursday and straightaway he was disappointed that I hadn't been at pickup earlier. He was sensitive about things like that. He might himself vanish for a week or two and reappear without warning or explanation, but it pained him when others did the same. He always feared the worst.

The worst, in his mind, was that the game should fall apart. We had held it together almost six years. That was a lifetime in pickup basketball. I found him afterward at Alphonse's. He was sitting alone at a table. He described for me how the games had been. Supposedly, he had been off all night, feeling clumsy and plodding on the court.

It was interesting that he would admit it; he could be quite hard on himself.

"I'll be there next week," I said. "Maybe the week after."

He didn't believe me. He would have to see the evidence.

The festival was coming up. It was a new period of summer, approaching the end. Soon we'd be back to playing nights at the Y with nowhere to have a drink afterward. The Y was a cold, cloistered building between the dump and the highway.

I began, in my own offhand manner, telling him what I was looking for. Mentioning that I was aware he had access to town boats. That they needed to be taken out now and again just to keep them seaworthy, and that he knew the harbor and the bay and could navigate them quietly, without signals or lights.

"What the fuck are we talking about?" he asked finally, sitting up in his chair.

The chairs were meant to look like wrought iron. The paint flaked and stuck to your skin.

"I need a boat," I said. "And someone to man it."

"A captain?"

I hesitated over the word. It didn't cost anything, but you could tell it meant a lot to him.

"Yes, a captain," I said. "A night job. I don't have the date yet. Soon, in all likelihood."

"For you and your dad? You're moving someone?"

"We don't move anyone over the water."

"You don't? I never knew that. So, what is it then?"

"A job. You want it? It's something new. You wanted change, right?"

He had more questions just then. They were very specific questions, as though he had been waiting quite a long time for me to ask him onto something I was working and had prepared a checklist in anticipation. Or else he was just being careful. He knew more about boats than I was expecting. I had a vague memory of one of his uncles owning a scallop boat before the fleet disbanded. Maybe Tommy used to go with him.

"Forget it," I said. "Really, I don't want you to worry. Forget I mentioned it."

"I'm not worried," he said. "I'm just asking, for Chrissake. Can't a guy ask?"

I told him I didn't want to talk through particulars. It was important that I not.

"I need a boat," I said. "And someone who can take the thing out without sinking it."

"Well, that's not true," he said. "You need someone with a boat who doesn't mind working on short to nonexistent fucking notice. And doing it quietly. And doing it without complaining that he's not being told what he's up to, or why, or how come there's not more money going into his pocket. Try another captain, see what he says."

We hadn't mentioned money yet. I guess he'd already begun the negotiations.

In any case, he knew that I could go to anyone in town with a boat. He was just enjoying himself, talking through the situation. He really did have an optimistic spirit.

I thought about how many times we had played ball together over the years. How it felt, coming down with a rebound: like I already knew where he'd be, though I hadn't looked for him and his movements were often erratic, like an animal's.

I had mentioned to Elena who I had in mind for transport and she gave pause but eventually acquiesced and said that was my area, she would trust me if I was sure. I wasn't sure, but I liked the idea nonetheless and it was a simple thing we were asking.

"I don't know about Goose Neck," Tommy said later, after we had already agreed and moved on to other subjects and ordered a bucket of beer, on me, for the guys who were still lingering around after the game, standing against the wall counter, not wanting to go home to whatever was waiting for them there. "That's a piece of work, out there."

"What do you mean?" I asked.

"I mean, you ever been? Really been out there?"

"Sure, why?"

"I don't know. It's just, it's fucking closed up, you know what I mean? You get a bad feeling walking around out there. Like you're trapped. That's what they want."

"Who does?"

"They, them, those people. The lords and ladies."

"When were you ever in Goose Neck?"

"You don't even want to know."

"I'm asking. It might be important."

He tensed up suddenly. He didn't want to cost himself the job. We had agreed to the pay, but it wasn't about money.

"This stays here," he said, leaning in. "Back in my, you know—not my salad days, the other fucking days, right?— back then, I used to go around to houses checking on cabinets. One time I was out there, in Goose Neck, at some fucking house, dark as death and middle of winter but I got into a big one, and I'm walking around thinking, Hell, there must be five bathrooms in this place, maybe more, and somebody's gonna leave something behind in one of them. Middle of the night, right? Middle of winter. Lights, none. Heat, none. And I'm minding my own business when some fucking guy comes walking out in pajamas. You know those old-time pajamas, with, like, the hats?"

"The Scrooge pajamas."

"Right, the fucking Scrooge pajamas. And he says, voice all low and like he's been sitting up at night swallowing pennies and dimes. Asks, may he help me. All calmness."

I waited for him to go on. He needed a moment. The memory had shaken him.

"Just like that," he said. "May I help you? Like he really wanted to, you know? I bolted fucking out of there faster than a mouse with a battery pack on his balls. And my ride, outside, he's gone. I don't know what spooked him but he's all the way gone, so I have to walk home and there's only that one road, you know? And I started thinking, Who was that guy? The guy in the pajamas. Best I could figure it, he was some kind of butler."

"What do you mean, a butler?"

"Like maybe everyone in the house was dead."

"Dead?"

"Right, dead, but the butler just kept on going. Doing his job. Helping people."

"Why would he do that?"

"Because that's what they do out in those big fucking houses. With the butlers and every other fucking person who makes the mistake of coming in. They carve into you."

He was leaning almost all the way over the table. His face, a few inches from mine.

I didn't know what to say. It seemed such an intense and personal experience. There was no point in trying to convince him of anything other than what he had already felt.

We were both quiet for a time. Tommy settled back into his seat again. He wanted another beer.

"Well, you won't have to go to shore," I said. "You can stay in the boat."

That boosted his spirit immediately. He was like another man altogether. A man who had never lived those darker days and had never had any winter run-ins with butlers.

We talked for a while about the festival. It was coming up soon and it was likely to interrupt our pickup game, but it also meant the end of summer. Tommy's schedule was lighter in the fall. Summer was his busiest time, and he was always worrying over small things like which movies to show in the band shell. It had never occurred to me that somebody was responsible for choosing the movies. It seemed roughly the same lineup played every year, except sometimes they showed *Jaws* twice.

Apparently, it wasn't so easy as that. The week before they had shown *The Friends of Eddie Coyle*. They didn't normally show movies with rough language, but Tommy had thought it would be all right because most of the language came from Robert Mitchum and because the movie was about Massachusetts and was filmed in towns south of Boston. There were complaints about it though, about the language and the theme.

"Look," he said. "You can trust me. I'm glad you came to me for this, Jack. I mean it."

"I know, Tommy."

"And maybe this is the kind of thing I'm supposed to do, you know? Could be, right?"

"Sure, you never know until you try it."

"I mean, I chose the movie, didn't I? Maybe it's fate."

"Maybe."

"Well, you're getting me in the action. I appreciate that. I won't fucking forget it."

He reached his hand over and pinched the skin inside his elbow. It looked like it hurt.

"I'm trying not to swear so much," he said. "After Eddie Coyle and everything."

I tried remembering the movie. I couldn't remember anything except for Mitchum looking tired, but for some reason I didn't believe there was all that much cursing in it.

17

We were at Marianne's and had been for some time, drinking out of coconut glasses, alternating between soda water and rum, both of them served with plenty of ice, while the Red Sox fell further and further behind in the first leg of a doubleheader that was making up for a June rain delay against the Tigers. Marianne was sitting on top of the bar, watching the game with her legs crossed rather primly. Whenever the tension rose, she would lift one sneaker onto the brass bar and tuck her knee under her chin, then eventually she would get up to walk once around the bar and return to precisely the same position.

The Sox were down five. The game as good as lost. She didn't seem to believe it, or maybe she did, but because it was the first of two legs, she was still holding on to some speck of hope. Elena said I should watch her closely. The superstition was more than that, she believed. It was ritual, and between those two abstract concepts was an ocean of possibility and significance. She had great affection for Marianne, as Marianne had for her. At some point around the sixth inning, Elena began telling me about her safecracker. She knew it was trite, needing something like that, but there was no getting around it. She had reasoned through her plan a hundred different ways. At the end of all of them, there was still a wall safe with a combination lock and reinforced steel. She would need to get inside it.

"Is there any peripheral security?" Marianne asked. Her eyes were on the screen still.

Elena shook her head. "One man, nothing rigged. No sensors, no traps."

"And what's the lock? Group two?"

"I don't know yet. Will it matter very much?"

Marianne laughed. She had a brief, tired laugh. Always the same, no matter the joke. She looked up at the portrait of Pedro Martínez in front of her on the wall. I remembered how she used to watch him when he was still pitching for the Sox: the way she insisted on utter silence while the ball was in his glove, and then she would start to hum as he went into his windup, and the humming would build until the ball came whipping out of his hand, and then she would sigh, and it would all begin again. That was during close games. Other times, when he was cruising, she would begin to cry.

Real, honest to God tears of joy. I had never seen anyone cry like that, except for her.

"Will it matter?" Marianne said. "A group-two lock, three wheels, a million combinations. Four wheels, a hundred million. Two hours of number cracking or twenty minutes if you want it done with tools. If it's a group-one lock and you don't want it broken, you're looking at a day and a half of work. Hard, concentrated work. Or you try to burn it. Even with a torch you'll be at it for half an hour and liable to burn the house down around it. There are so many different locks, sweetie. The particulars matter."

I tried remembering a bit of what was in Marianne's past but came up with nothing much except the names of various port cities on the maritime Silk Road. An interesting woman.

My father had always kept a respectful distance from her. Nodding hello as she passed.

Marianne spun herself around so that she faced us.

"I could use an underwriter's report," she said. "Something from a lab, if you have it."

Elena smiled and shook her head. "Can't get it for you. Don't have it."

"An owner's manual."

"Long gone, I'm afraid. This safe's older than I am. I'd say by about a decade."

Marianne nodded gravely. I was nearly invisible to them, it seemed. "Pictures, then."

"I'll do my best."

"Use film. I don't want to look at pixels."

"Good. Film, and we'll burn the negatives after. Jack's got the old spy cameras."

They turned to me for the first time and I smiled. It was true, I did have spy cameras. My father's old collection, mostly of Soviet and Eastern European models, the ancients.

"Is that why I'm along?" I asked.

"Everybody has to bring something to the table," Elena said.

We all went back to watching the Red Sox for a while. It looked as though they might claw back into the game but then gave away a rally. Four more runs in the eighth. Marianne left the bar without a word and Elena and I were the only ones there.

We got up and went to the back porch, which was filled with cigarette butts from the night before. Across the bluffs, the wind was shifting, and it felt like a new warmth was reaching the town. A fast-moving system from the southeast, something almost tropical.

"I've always wanted to see her work," she said. "I've only seen it in pieces."

"I didn't know she did that sort of thing."

"Oh sure, forever. I used to come around to clean this place when I was a kid. Before you knew me. I'd come in on Saturdays and Sundays. She has a safe upstairs in the office and she asked me if I wanted to see something. We went upstairs and she got out all her little pencils and chits. Took apart a group-two lock and showed me how. It isn't like you think. It's all these fine little markings on the paper, and it's long, slow, deliberate work. If you're going to crack it. If you're going to break it, it's brute force. Still beautiful, and I'd love to see how she'd manage that too. A delicate woman like that. Six hundred pounds of pressure. That's what a group-one lock can absorb. But she'd manufacture it somehow, don't you think? It would be so lovely to see her do it."

"Is that the plan? She cracks the safe, I keep everyone busy, and you admire her at it?"

"Don't be crass, Jack. You're talking about a perfect world."

"That's your perfect world?"

"Oh that, and plenty of ice cream that never melts. Look, I have a confession to make."

"What's that?"

"Around your house, that day, a couple weeks ago, with Javi . . ."

"The Galician Venezuelan. The gigolo."

"Right, him. I was snooping."

"Snooping for what?"

"A name. One of your old clients breaks into safes, doesn't he? Or used to?"

She was leaning over the rail, looking out toward the harbor. How had she known that?

"Hector," I said. "He was an activist in the old days. And a locksmith."

"Hector," she said. "I hadn't known his name. But I thought, well—I don't know what I thought. That you left ledgers lying around the house. Something very old-fashioned, listing everyone's names and numbers and addresses and assorted criminal expertise."

"That night with the Vizconde de Triacastela?"

"Javi, yes."

"But you already had Marianne."

She sighed. "I was nervous. What if she said no? What if she told me it was idiotic?"

She sounded so genuinely worried, I couldn't answer. Sincerity unmans me.

"Anyway," she said. "I just wanted you to know. It was a lousy thing to do, snooping."

"That's all right. Did you find anything interesting?"

"Just the spy cameras. Do they really work?"

"Yes. They're Soviet bloc. Nothing ever dies from there."

"Do you know how to use them?"

"Sure, anybody could."

"That's good. We'll need to take some pictures. It's all very exciting, isn't it?"

There was that tone again. Again, it caught me off guard and I didn't answer her.

LATER, I WENT OUT the side door and crossed the bluffs. The scent of sea plum blooms still lingered in the air and a flower that smelled like jasmine but wasn't jasmine. I had never been able to figure out what it was, but it bloomed in summer. For some reason, I never wanted to ask anyone who would know. It was good to keep a few mysteries around, in case you needed them. More wildflowers were blooming along the Jersey fence, so that was where I walked until I came to the band shell. It was around ten o'clock. There was a performance going. A woman singing, accompanied by a violin, guitar, and keyboard. She had bright eyes that soaked up the stage lights, and she was sweating a great deal. The billing said that her name was Vera Baptiste. I sat down on one of the benches to listen.

She was singing morna. There's no simple way to describe morna to somebody who hasn't heard it. It's tavern music, related to fado from Portugal. Anguished strings and plaintive vocals. The songs are always about home and experiences lost to time and wondering what your old friends and lovers are up to. The arrangements tend to be simple and the rhythm holds steady, built around fifths, but a good band creates with the strings a sensation of doom that's nearly overwhelming. You almost can't bear to listen. All exile ballads are about fate, but with morna you get the feeling there's no end to pain, only cycles like the tides. She sang a few in Creole. One was about Tarrafal. Tarrafal was the prison camp Salazar opened on Cape Verde. It sounded like she knew about it. She was around my age, or maybe older, but too young to have been there herself. Maybe someone in her family had been. I had never heard the song, and I knew before she was done, it was the kind of song that would stay with me for a long time afterward.

18

We went through the cameras the next night. It was a small collection, but it had meant a lot to my father once. Then, like other things that had meant something to him, he cast them aside as staunchly as he gathered them. They had to be removed from his house at once or he was going to drop them at the dump. He was never entirely committed, except that he held a deep, unwavering respect for his whims and it made him feel good to act on them briskly, without reservation. It was all those years in the service, being told what to do maybe. He liked reminding himself he was his own lord.

The cameras were kept in a steamer trunk that had been outfitted with three levels of shelves and lined with satin. There were several different models of Zorki, which the Soviets had designed to look and operate similar to the German-made Leica. My favorite was the Zorki 4, and I showed Elena how you set the shutter speed after you were done winding it, and she agreed that, for some reason neither of us could define, it was the most satisfying way to do it. It was a bulky camera compared with some of the spy vehicles and the slip-knot lenses and matchboxes, but she said that was the one we should use.

It felt like a game. So much so that I no longer particularly regretted missing pickup that week or the week before. Lately a feeling of restlessness had gripped me, and she had seemed to absorb it the way another person sometimes can—but only for a short burst before it belonged all to me again. That's what I was thinking about, and she was outside on the porch, playing with the cameras, aiming them across the street at the old public boat launch and at the gulls circling overhead, maybe with clams or crabs they were about to break open on the pavement. It all depended on the moon, I was pretty sure. During certain moons, the male fiddler crabs came out of their dens and sawed their big pincer claws in the soft light for the benefit of the females, and while they were out there performing, the gulls would come to snatch them up. Other times, the gulls only ate clams. I never knew which phase we were in.

Elena kept working with the cameras. I could hear the shutters going and sometimes there would be a flash. Mostly she was working without any light, or with very little. Give her another hour and she would have the whole trunk mastered. She could pick things up and figure them out so quickly, it was a little intimidating. It made you feel simple and slow, or comical.

While we were working through the options, she asked what I wanted to do with the money. Somehow it wasn't something we had discussed before. My cut was generous. More money than I'd ever considered, and enough so as to seem almost unreal.

Assuming we did it. Assuming she could sell them afterward. That it wasn't a game.

"I'm not going to let you have it if you give it all away to churches," she said.

"I won't give them anything."

"You promise?"

"I'm going to leave," I said. "I'm moving away."

The statement hung between us for what seemed like a very long time.

"Are you really?" she asked.

"Yes."

"Where are you going?"

"Paris."

She laughed. A clipped laugh that nearly came out of her nose. "Paris?"

"Sure, I could go to Paris. Why not?"

"Are you going to be a painter or a dancer or what?"

"I could paint. Hell, I could work as an artist's model."

"You could do anything, Jack. I'd never doubt you."

A while later, after we were sitting down again, she said she wished I would go to Paris.

"I'm serious about it," I said. "I'm leaving. Once you sell the diamonds, I'm gone."

"No, you're not serious. I wish that you were, Jack. You might think that you are."

"Why shouldn't I be?"

"What happens to your father?"

"I'll leave him provided for and then some."

"And the business?"

"I don't care what happens to the business. That's the point of being in Paris, right?"

"That's true. You've got it all figured out. Still, I wish that you were serious."

"Stop saying that, would you?"

"I will. Sorry, Jack. Only it's a lot of money. You could do anything."

"The same for you. What are you planning for it? I guess you've got it all figured out."

"Me? Christ, no. Why would I have?"

"I thought that's what people did when they stole something big."

"You're thinking of the movies, Jack. Where they carry little collages around in their pockets to tell you about the beaches where they're going to go to die. Just one last job."

She mimed something in the darkness. Taking a paper out of her pocket maybe.

"It has nothing to do with money," she said. "You know that, don't you? I hope you do."

"Sure. I do."

"I mean it. I want you to know that."

I told her again that I did. I thought that I meant it too. It was a nice night and I didn't want to spoil anything.

19

On Saturday, I was coming back from a supply run to Philadelphia, carrying more money than I liked having around and most of it hidden in the wheel wells. Anyone searching for it would look in the wheel wells, especially on a Wrangler, which had a lot of space there, enough for a duffel bag if that's how you wanted to carry it. Half the money was getting dropped into the trunk of a Hyundai Sonata in the parking lot outside the Dartmouth Olive Garden. I'd been there to eat once, when I was young. I hadn't thought about the place in years, but sitting around outside it waiting for the Hyundai to show up, I started thinking about the breadsticks and the pasta e fagioli, which I had ordered, pronouncing it like I was from New Jersey because that was the only way I had ever heard it pronounced. With half the money gone I felt better, lighter.

I was thinking about how easy it would be simply to take the other half. The idea frightened me, although it really would have been simple. A quarter million, vanished.

That was when Elena called. I was driving toward New Bedford on 195, a drive she and I had made together many dozens of times. I was coming up on the sign for the old dog park, with the mechanical greyhound lifted way up over the highway and the lights flashing underneath like legs. She asked if I wanted to go to a party. I said I'd pick her up in an hour. I wanted to drop off the money first. She told me to bring the camera.

Later, she was waiting for me on the curb, wearing long black slacks, cuffed above the ankles, and a light sweater. I had never seen her dressed like that before.

We crossed over the Bourne Bridge and took County Road for a while. It was old Cape in there. Foundation stones dug from the earth and well-water connections. The old Cape was something different, whether you were in Chatham or Sandwich or on the Vineyard or Naushon, for that matter. I had never been to Naushon but I knew the stories. It was the island where the Forbeses went in summer. They brought their friends from Yale and rode horses and put on plays. The men would perform the old rites, the same as they performed them in Kennebunkport and one or two other places around New England. It was old spy country, when you got down to it. Not spies like my father but like the men who had decided where he would go and whether he would live or be sacrificed. The men who set themselves up for wars twenty years in advance and had the right interests in place and their sons positioned for Congress afterward. Their time had passed. Everyone knew it except for them, and that was what made them dangerous. It was their ignorance and their greed, which was like a dampness in the air.

The old railroad line was running alongside us. It was overgrown in stretches. We crossed the tracks near Monument Beach and found the way. There was only the one road servicing Goose Neck and a lot of small blind lanes and dead ends spilling from it.

"They're always giving parties," she said. "They're afraid what'll happen if they stop spinning. On weekends they like to bring in young people. They think of me as young."

We parked along the dirt lane on the left shoulder. I made a three-point turn and left the Jeep facing north, toward the road. You could get the ignition started with a flathead screwdriver if you were ever in a pinch. There were cars on both shoulders. We walked toward the gate, and when we got there Elena knew the code to punch into the pad. Beside the gate was a stone fence about two and a half to four feet high in places that ran into the woods until you couldn't follow it. There was another dirt path up to the house. From the rear it looked modest and you could hardly distinguish it from the trees, though I remembered what it had looked like from the water. We went around the side.

It was a captain's cottage, perched atop a hill overlooking the bay. In late afternoon, the sun's glare off the water would have been blinding. At that hour of night, there were lights from each of the villages and together they traced a seam along the Cape's southern flank. That was Falmouth and Woods Hole. You could see out to Naushon, too, but there were no lights there. You knew only that there was an island in the darkness.

Elena walked ahead. I kept a step behind. The grass was patchy and damp.

"They call it a salon," she said. "Try to meet somebody interesting. I'll find you later."

On the back lawn, there were games set up. I wasn't expecting that. I didn't know what, exactly, I was expecting. A woman came over to say hello to Elena and they went off together toward one of the games, and I went alone to the bar. There was another bar inside the house. There was always another bar in the house. That one on the lawn was fine. The soda bottles were flat because the caps had been left off earlier, but I didn't want any soda or tonic with my drink. There were sandwiches too. They were spread out on a platter covered with plastic wrap. The glasses were all cut crystal.

It had been a long time since I'd gone to a party on the Cape. In college, there were weekend caravans. You would end up at somebody's uncle's cottage. They always called them cottages no matter the size. It had to do with the manner in which they were used.

The crowd there didn't look so young to me, though it might have to the Paulsons. There were about sixty people spread out across the lawn. Most of them seemed to know one another. Or was it only because I was alone and wandering around that it appeared that way? I caught sight of Frank Paulson, playing host. He looked like a country squire dressed in ratty chinos and a plaid shirt, wearing New Balance sneakers. It was a uniform you found all over the Cape, like they were farmers on market day.

He was huddled with a small group, explaining something

to them. There were likely clients in attendance, or prospective clients. They were impossible to pick out. That was the point of throwing the party. You never knew who might need legal advice one day or whose friends would need it, and they would think of you when they did. In the meantime, you would mix them with a lot of other people: friends and third cousins and a few artists. They would all feel indebted in the great obscure ledger the old New England families kept, always making payments and withdrawals and collecting chits off one another. It was the same in other places, only here it went back hundreds of years and you paid for parties your grandfather had been to. The artists were part of it. They were subsidized by the Paulsons and their friends. Fellowships and colonies. Room and board on the coast for a summer, and all you had to do was go to a few parties and drink gin with lawyers and insurance men. It was old Cape bullshit. The weather was good, and they thought that God had chosen them for it.

A man who was watching one of the games came over to where I was standing and introduced himself. He was a novelist. His name was Henderson. He paused after saying it, hoping you might recognize him. He was on the Cape on some kind of fellowship. He thought I might be a writer too. There were a lot of writers there at the party and some painters also. He didn't know anyone, but he wanted to meet a painter.

"I don't know what people paint nowadays," he said. "I'd like to find out."

I told him I didn't know either. I was sorry not to be able to help.

He shrugged and started walking away, then turned back

and filled up his glass with vodka. "What I'd really like," he said, "is to meet one who paints religious themes. All anyone used to paint was religion, but now I don't know what the hell they're up to. Maybe they still think it's religious. That's what I'd like to find one for. To ask about it."

After he found some ice for his vodka, he went off to discuss it with some other people.

I went inside the house. The bar was in the kitchen. All the soda there was fresh and unopened, and beside a carved silver ice bucket there were shakers that looked antique.

The family portraits were on the wall. Generations of upright lawyers and parsons.

The two security men were hanging around outside. Kalianidis and the other, whose name was Maloney, sitting in a beach chair in the shade beneath an elm tree. He looked like a valet or a caterer on smoke break. They both wore earpieces and were studying the guests. Occasionally one of them would look to the horizon and shield his eyes. Neither went into the house. It was a pleasant evening, if slightly warm and still.

The safe was in the den. Where the den was, that was a mystery, but it wasn't a large house so much as a rambling one, with a certain erratic logic of its own. Soon I had found my way down a dark hallway, running fingers along the old wooden walls.

A pantry. A maid's room, outfitted now with bunk beds. Then, it was there, unlocked.

It was a room somewhat out of place, out of context. Halfheartedly dedicated to work. There were more paintings on the walls. Bookshelves, two armchairs, and a large desk made of mahogany. The paintings were seascapes, all of them stormy. A few portraits of flat-nosed seamen in formal collars with identical hairlines. I turned on a light. There was no point using a flashlight and making a show of myself as a cat burglar if I was caught. Better to plead ignorance. Lost on the way to the bathroom. Curious about something in the room. Cape architecture and design.

There was a painting of an old whaler coming into port, with a storm chasing behind. It was hanging slightly crooked.

The safe was behind it. I took the painting off its hooks and leaned it against the wall and began to work.

No flattery, no story about drunken misadventures on the way to the bathroom would be able to explain what I was doing with a painting off the wall, so I worked quickly and began sweating. There was nothing I could ever do about sweat and I had long since ceased to be embarrassed by it. There was no point being embarrassed over an element, over a piece of your body. It could fluster you some, but only if you allowed it.

Voices behind me, in the hall. I put the camera down, then froze, unsure about what to do next. They passed, and I went back to it for five or six more shots and called it.

It was satisfying work. Simple chemical work. Light burned onto film. I thought about what Elena had said about the gravitational pull, but I didn't feel that. The diamonds were inside the safe, or maybe they weren't, but what I liked was taking those photographs.

On my way out of the room, I tried remembering the details

so that I could draw blueprints later. Then figured I would take some shots of the entryway and the hall too.

My first time casing a robbery. I went outside, back to the Jeep, and left the camera. There was a lockbox in the center console. Not such great security, but it would do fine.

I thought maybe we would leave now that it was done, but I couldn't find her straightaway. The woman who had pulled Elena aside when we first came in saw me and took my arm. She was one of those people, born jailers, who are always taking you into custody. Something red, like fruit juice, had stained the sides of her lips and her teeth.

"Hey, you're Elena's friend," she said. "We've got to stick together. I know everyone here. You've got to save me from them. You're the only one I can talk to. Really talk to."

We went to a swing hanging underneath an elm tree. She was guiding us. I would have had to remove her hand from my arm finger by finger to get free. She told me her name was Hayes. I didn't know if that was her first name or last or just something people called her. "I want you to tell me everything," she said. "What was she like when she was young? She never tells stories. Deflects with questions. Were you in love with her?"

I told her I didn't know her when she was young.

"But I thought you grew up together," she said.

"No, that must be somebody else."

She seemed so disappointed. Her head slumped down on my shoulder.

"You'll be at the wedding, won't you? I'll need someone to keep me honest. I'll know everyone there, too, and it'll be awful if I don't have someone keeping me honest the whole time. I'm fun at weddings though. You'll see. Just give me a chance. Only I wonder why they're not having it on the Vineyard. You know Mike. He lets his aunts do the shopping. I guess they wanted a city wedding. God forbid they cross the family."

She said a few more things about Mike. She seemed to know all about him but hadn't seen him in a while. At some point, she got up and wandered into the neighbor's yard.

I STARTED GETTING DRUNK. I hadn't been drunk in a long time. It wasn't something I imposed on myself, just an ingrained pragmatism. There was plenty of gin at the bar. That was what I started with. It burned a path down your throat for the next to follow.

The party kept going. Drinks trays were emptied and then freshened. A station wagon pulled into the driveway and unloaded some people and took others away and went back out through the gate like a shuttle service. You could see the headlights moving through the trees. The high beams were on and whoever was driving was taking the Goose Neck roads gingerly. Roads in those villages were in terrible condition, as a rule.

An old dog wandered through the yard. It didn't seem to live there. Someone had brought him. He was a Doberman and had that cold swagger like all German dogs, but there was a sweetness about him too. He was carrying a plush toy in his mouth. A small gray rabbit, something meant for a child. He wanted you to be impressed with it.

I played with him for a while. Admired his toy. Took it from him and gave it back.

The novelist, Henderson, picked me out again. He was irrepressible.

All that time he had been looking for painters to interrogate, or so he claimed.

"I talked to one," he said. "She paints psychosexual landscapes. No religion at all."

"Did she show you any?"

He nodded. "On her phone. Not bad. They sorta look like apple orchards."

He thought that was pretty funny. He repeated it, in case I hadn't heard.

"So what do you do?" he asked after the joke, if that's what it was, had worn off.

"I help people hide, then I move them wherever they need to go next."

"There much money in that?"

"Some."

"Steady work?"

"Like painting landscapes. It comes and goes."

"Seasonal. That's never easy."

"I'm getting into other things."

"Oh yeah? Branching out. That's smart, I guess." He shrugged sadly and seemed to be looking around for another drink. "I'd like to work with my hands. Build a house, room by room. Ever do that?"

He started waving his hands around in the air. Building something invisible.

"Our fathers built houses," he went on. "Hell, say what you want about psychosexual landscapes, but at least she's working with her hands, right? Jesus, am I tired though."

He went over to a game of cornhole, knelt beside the board, and knocked on the wood. Testing it maybe. Deciding whether he could use the lumber. A woman knelt down beside him. She might have been his wife or girlfriend, but I didn't think so.

I kept up with the gin and it didn't seem so dangerous. None of it did. The games were even fun. I played one for a while where you threw a foot-long rope that was weighted on either end and tried wrapping it around a three-rung ladder. I didn't know what it was called. I kept an eye on Elena too. She was talking with just about everyone there. They wanted to be near her, to make her laugh. It occurred to me that she could disappear into those people forever. They were inviting her to. It would have been easy.

The night went on and you felt a little younger with each hour that passed. I watched some people start dancing. They danced around a pole, then one of them fell and tripped the others she was with and they stayed on the grass sharing a cigarette, passing it around and blowing smoke on one another. Everyone was drinking a great deal. Summer was far along. August. The heat wasn't letting up, but it would someday.

I switched over to tonic water but it was too late and I would have to ride out the gin. That was fine, there were plenty of people around and they were all more or less drunk.

At one point, I got the impression Frank Paulson was watching me. Maybe it was because I hadn't gone to talk with him earlier. I should have. Etiquette mattered. He wasn't wearing a ring, but you were meant to find something to kiss and to do it gently.

Finally, he came over. He had taken off his New Balance sneakers and was barefoot. Hands in his pockets like he was out for a stroll after dinner, digesting and ruminating.

"Are you having a good time?" he asked.

"Yes," I said. "Thanks for having me."

He grinned and nodded. It was meant to be a folksy interaction. Affable. Curious.

His eyes narrowed a little. They were blue eyes, not kind exactly but innocent.

"I've seen you before," he said. "I've been trying to figure out where. Remind me."

"I don't think we've met."

"No, I don't mean that. But I'm good with faces."

Somebody stopped to say goodbye. He asked after her parents, then turned back.

"I never forget one," he said. "That's my cross to bear."

It seemed he was waiting for me to tell him mine. I smiled and drank my tonic.

His wife came over, Billie Paulson, weekly resident of the Sam'l Allen Inn.

Elena was with her. Smiling, glad to see me. They were holding on to each other. The older woman was all angles and sharp edges and looked as though she'd been called sporty when she was young, and this had solidified in her and shaped everything to come.

"This is my wife, Billie," Paulson said.

He asked her to confirm he was good with faces. It meant a lot to him.

"He's not as sharp as he used to be," she said. "He was a needle when he was young."

"I'm still plenty sharp," he said.

The word *sharp* brought out their accents. I got the feeling that was why they said it.

"Jack is an old friend," Elena said. "I've known him forever. I'm so glad you two met."

Paulson was looking at me carefully, studying me. Rolling onto his heels and toes as he did, working the grass and the soil into his soles. I didn't know why he'd taken his shoes off, but it looked pleasant walking around that way, with your pant legs rolled up.

"Harvard basketball," he said finally. Proud of himself, like an ace student.

He wanted to shake hands. We had already done it before, but he wanted to shake again.

"We were what that year?" he asked. "Seven and seven?"

He meant our Ivy League record. Those were the games that mattered to some people.

He had put himself on the team very casually with that we. Maybe he was a booster.

"Three and eleven," I said.

"Dammit, was it that bad? You never remember them that bad."

"No, I guess you don't."

He looked to his wife. "I told you," he said. "Still sharp. You doubted me."

"Never," she said.

"You did. Elena never would, but you did. For a moment. It's all right."

Elena shook her head. Pretending to indulge them both. To be amused by them.

But I saw something in her eyes. It was worry, I thought. Not quite panic but close.

"What are you doing these days?" Paulson asked.

"He's a lawyer," Elena said. "Local counsel."

"Is that right?" He was looking at me with open skepticism. Trying to remember something more. "What's the practice like down here?" he asked.

"A lot of wills," I said. "Old ladies leaving houses to their dogs. Traffic violations."

He nodded like I had told him something very important or confidential. Then, you could see it coming to him, the thing he had been trying to remember. One thing more.

"You work with your father," he said. "I remember hearing that. The alumni circuit."

"My father's not an alumnus."

"No," he said. "He isn't. But you two work together, don't you? I remember it now."

He was proud of himself. Turning to Billie, smiling, giving nothing else away.

Elena suppressing herself too. All of us withholding. A very Cape conversation.

"You get to do much sailing?" he asked.

It seemed such an odd question, but he didn't think so, or was pretending not to.

"No," I said.

"You still play ball?"

"Pickup games. Local. Nothing organized."

"How are your knees? I always worry about a fellow's knees."

I told him they were okay, and he asked several other questions, mostly about basketball. I answered them as well as I could. It felt like a deposition, and I didn't want to say anything I might contradict later. Billie left to get drinks and soon came back with something that had a name. A drink she had invented herself. It tasted like Mountain Dew and maybe had some mixed in. She had a tray of them and wanted you to try one.

"Every summer she designs a new drink," Paulson said. It sounded like he admired her. "Excuse us," he added, taking the tray from her. "Let's talk more ball later."

For a while, Elena didn't speak and didn't move and it was like the world had stopped.

"I take it you weren't planning on that," I said.

"That he'd know you? No, I suppose I wasn't."

We walked over to the bar and each poured a drink. Gin for me, rum for her.

She was thinking things through. You could almost hear it, standing beside her.

"It doesn't need to change anything," she said. "It might change something. I don't know yet. I'll have to work on it. I was thinking you'd come in fresh and be something different. Diversion, you know? Misdirection. You don't mind me saying that, do you, Jack? Christ, this is new though. So he knows you. Remembers you. Knows your father, too, it seems like.

That's not ideal. If he knows your father and knows you work with him, he's going to figure something's up. His guard will be up like it wouldn't have been otherwise. That's fine though. We can use all that somehow."

She wasn't asking me how. She wasn't asking me anything at all. Her mind was going.

But then I got the impression that it was for show. That she wasn't worried or panicked at all, but rather had decided, for reasons undisclosed—reasons that I couldn't yet guess at—to put on a kind of performance. Like she wanted me to believe that everything had suddenly gone to shit.

It was an ungenerous thought, but it occurred to me and there was no getting rid of it.

I went over to the hillside that dropped down to the bay and lay on the grass. Looking out at the lights playing on the water's surface, I wondered how much longer we would stay. It felt suddenly like we had been there for days. One of those weekend parties that never finish. You're trapped and all you want is a ride, but one never comes.

20

didn't hear from her for several days, and a rather distinct certainty began to settle onto me that our project was finished. Paulson had made me. It was something that didn't fit into her plan. She had worked it a hundred different ways. She told me that she had, and I tried believing. None of those hundred ways included getting made, so it was over. I walked around town and went for a long swim across the boating channel and into the mouth of the bay, where the water got cool and dark. After an hour, I came back into the harbor feeling I might not make it to shore. The current was strong. It wanted to pull you into open water. My chest began to throb, like it was tied with rope.

In town there was quite a lot of excitement and activity and new families arriving: turnover in the cottages, sometimes twice a week, although everyone wanted to stick around for the festival if they could. There were several minor celebrations but the largest was at the end of the month. That was when the social clubs would be out in the streets parading and candles were lit in churches. Carnival rides, numbers games, a great deal of music. The town's population nearly doubled week after week.

In years past it was the period of summer I liked best. Busy, like a train station at the end of the day, with all the bodies coming and going. It didn't feel that way to me anymore. In its place there was something new and I found myself thinking about people I had treated shabbily over the years. People who hadn't deserved it at all.

Then, on Tuesday afternoon, she called and told me we were on.

At first, I didn't understand. She didn't want to spell it out over the phone.

"Get the boat ready," she said. "Pick me up in the Jeep. He wants to play bridge."

"Bridge?"

"You know how."

"Jesus, I'd rather do anything else."

"Don't worry, I'll cover your losses. This is happening, Jack."

"Tonight?"

"Tonight."

It felt like a barometer was turning over. Something in the air was changing, invisible but real.

I spent the rest of the afternoon packing what was needed. It took three tries to get ahold of Tommy. He had the boat ready, waiting in a slip: a thirty-year-old twenty-five-foot whaler that the town had requisitioned and put to no particular purpose.

Sometimes park staff took kids out on it and called it marine biology. He had the dinghy too.

I made a production of not showing him what I was loading into the hold.

"I'm just the captain," he said. "Why bother telling me?"

"Just try not to hit any waves, you'll be fine."

"Waves, all right, smart-ass. I'll do that. Guy's got me hauling a fucking minefield."

He kept busy tying knots, then untying them. They were complicated knots and I wondered where he had learned them and why he had kept in practice. He was excited.

I checked his phone and set the alarms. We were going to fall silent. I wanted to make sure he understood. He had the times and the fallbacks. There were three fallbacks because you can't trust a boat. A dozen things might have held him in dock or in the marina longer than he would like, or he might be interrupted en route to Goose Neck.

He kept smiling as he recited the coordinates and the fallback times. He had a thin, crooked smile, like maybe he had teeth he wanted to hide or some other minor vanity.

"Don't worry," he said. That same line again. Everyone smiling, feeling good, ready.

I picked up Elena at six. She wanted to see them at the Sam'l Allen Inn first.

"We'll keep our distance," she said. "You know how to do it. I want to see the lovers, that's all. Wish them well. We'll ask our friend to send up champagne. A second bottle."

On the drive over, she kept fiddling with the radio. Looking for a station maybe.

Six thirty at this point. Not too many guests at the inn, from the looks of it.

From the road, you could see them out walking the grounds. Her, twenty-eight years older but not looking it. She kept herself fit, elegant. She was wearing a tailored pantsuit. They appeared to have already been up in the room. Just a feeling you got, seeing them. They walked hand in hand.

"They'll have two more goes at it," Elena said. It sounded like she knew for certain, though she couldn't have. "I'm glad for her. She deserves something nice."

"Seen enough?"

"I want this buttoned up, that's all. You can't blame me. We'll be exposed."

"How exposed?"

"You know as well as I do." After a pause, she went on. "Just a flash of skin."

On the drive back over to Goose Neck, I felt my pulse starting to quicken. Not with tension but with anticipation. I was glad we were heading there. Surprised it was beginning but glad for it and eager to see the gables on the rooftops through the trees.

"Park on the road," Elena said. "Same spot as last time. I know you're superstitious."

Paulson answered the door himself. There was nobody in the house except for him and the other guard, whose name was Patrick. Patrick Maloney, wearing a sweater and mixing cocktails like he had been living in a manor on the Upper Cape his whole life.

"I'm grateful to you," Paulson said. "Elena knows it. I can't be left to my own devices."

"Don't denigrate yourself, Frank," Elena said. "It rings false."

"Come in. We've got the run of the place. Get yourself fixed up."

Elena asked after Billie. Sounding surprised but not altogether disappointed.

"I'll tell her you asked," he said. "You're her favorite. Prefers you to me."

"False again."

"She tolerates me. A solid marriage, built on forbearance. It's harder than concrete."

He thought his wife was at a book club. Meetings held weekly throughout the summer, at a friend's house. He couldn't remember the friend's name but said she lived in Sandwich somewhere. "I had to send her with a driver," he said. "I don't want her coming home in pieces. I don't know how they get any reading done with what they drink."

The house appeared rather different in the light, without the people on the lawn or milling around inside looking for drinks and bathrooms. It felt older and more precarious. You could see some of the walls were flimsy. Additions made, rooms separated with no particular logic, satisfying the whim of some other branch of the family who had held it for a time. Everything old, tired. A shrine to a slightly dingy past, with the shelves full of knickknacks and the furniture looking worn and as though it might not last another summer. But it would. There was a grim determination to it all.

Inside the den, twenty feet from where we sat down at a card table made of maple, holding on to our drinks and with coasters and scorecards already set out, were the diamonds. Worth three million or a hundred and eighty million, depending on the tax authorities you were addressing. Worth somewhere in between those imaginary, meaningless figures once you took them quietly to market. Again, I tried feeling what Elena had described: the gravity of the act we were undertaking. It didn't quite come.

"Contract bridge is a weakness," Paulson said. "There's no other way to approach it."

We sat down and played for an hour or a little longer. He was partnered with Elena. A particular request. He said that playing with her was a treat because she was so wonderfully indirect. He must have meant about the signals, the betting, the contracts.

I had played bridge only a handful of times. Maloney seemed rather practiced. Maybe they had kept him at the table all summer and he was in fine late-season form, not needing to perform any calculations or watch for any signs but just ruthlessly going about the defenses and declarations and taking in more tricks than you expected him to.

There was a great deal of lingo. I always suspected that was why people played it.

The strategy, too, was opaque. Difficult to decipher, then, once you had, fairly simple.

Bridge of all pretenses was among the more preposterous, but we were in the door.

Paulson had asked for me, Elena said. She had known he would, once he found out where I went to college. Things like that meant a great deal to some people. On the Cape especially.

He had wanted the two of us to come over and keep him company, along with Maloney, who seemed so comfortable in that house but was still hired help.

Elena had things in hand. Probably she had been there for bridge other nights. While we played, she kept up the patter, as I had heard her that night at Monk Teller's, keeping five lonely men in a game of five-card straight through night into morning, without anyone losing his head or his money or feeling too cheated.

She was dealing crooked again, just like at Monk's, but her technique had improved.

I wouldn't have spotted it without knowing. She was talking all the time, asking questions like she was in a deposition. Probably they had done that before. Paulson thought of himself as her mentor. You could see it when they were together, that pride.

At her urging, he told a story about a client. Betraying secrets, quite freely.

I began wondering what else might be in the house. If he would keep rough diamonds worth some tens of millions in a wall safe, there must be other valuables secreted away.

Or maybe he was too cheap for all that. Every ten years, an estate sale, performed quietly, away from prying eyes, so that the brooches and cameos and candlesticks merely traded hands among the families who trafficked in that sort of forged history.

The game seemed to be moving so slowly. I thought for a time it was because I had figured out some essential piece of it and now the action was unfolding at its proper pace and my mind was digesting and analyzing it more swiftly, without effort, the way it happens with basketball and other games. But it was too soon for that. I was still barely finding my way through the contracts. It was just Elena controlling the pace. When she was dealing and when she wasn't. It felt like all of us were playing on strings.

Just after sundown she pushed her chair back. The house was getting dark. There were hardly any lights, though there were a great many clocks. Nine that I counted. Antiques.

"I'll need a few minutes," she said, standing up. "Nobody minds if I abandon ship?"

She was the dummy and had turned over her cards for Paulson to play.

A string of spades in her hand. It lit something in his eyes.

"Go on," he said. "Fix yourself another. Fix me one. Walk the grounds. Go for a swim. I've got these contracts sewn up, my dear. All their defenses, I assure you, will die ingloriously on the vine. If you come back through the kitchen, could you pick up ice?"

I checked my watch. I didn't like wearing a watch or anything on my hands or wrists, and if I could have gotten away without carrying a phone, I would have done it. It was ten past eight. All nine clocks in the room read something different. A few were frozen, and the others were wrong. Just then Marianne would be walking down the marina stairs, or maybe she would be on the boat already, and Tommy would be trying his damnedest not to make conversation with her because he wanted to seem professional but would be curious all the same. Wondering how long she had been in this line of work. As far as I knew, he never went to her bar. They may as well have been strangers.

Or they were already on the water. I hoped they were. Elena had moved a little early.

"Did you ever play at the Lion's Ass?" Paulson asked. He was looking at his cards.

It sounded like gibberish or code. He looked up at me through the glasses he had deigned to wear after his second drink. They were reading glasses, but you got the feeling he needed something stronger.

"I don't think I know it," I said.

"In back of Emerson. It's what they called it in my day. A long time ago. Just a place for spoiled boys to throw away money. Good for you, if you weren't in the habit. I got the bug for a year. Ran through half a semester's expenses in a weekend. You play well though. Like you learned young. It's not going to save you now, but it's still admirable."

He was feeling bolstered by the cards. Safe and having himself a time.

It was clever of Elena to set things up that way. I didn't ask but presumed that she had planted the suggestion of bridge in his mind and he had insisted on making a foursome.

A Tuesday night, when his wife was away at book club. With the guard. Wearing her white pantsuit. While he was at home having his three stiff drinks, about to be robbed.

He told a story about the Lion's Ass. It had to do with money won and lost but it seemed only to hold together in his memory. Eventually he gave up on the details and went back to his hand. Those spades, still making him smile. He'd hardly had to play any of them. Maloney was ready to give up.

I checked my watch again. She had been gone for twelve minutes. Longer than I had thought she would be, but then I didn't know much about bridge, or about its etiquette.

Minutes kept passing. All of it happening more slowly than I had imagined.

She came back with ice in a silver bucket and new drinks for the table. Nodding to me as she did, an almost impercep-tible gesture but reassuring all the same. Paulson finished out the round and topped out his bid by three tricks. He added it to the scorecard.

The way he kept score was somewhat byzantine. Not on a grid but in snaking rows.

Elena shuffled the cards. She was doing it often, to keep things moving between hands.

None of the rest of us could manage it half as smoothly and there was something mesmerizing about watching her do it. Paulson really did look proud, playing with her.

"We'll send you to the Las Vegas office," he said. "Next year, remind me. Make a note."

"A Las Vegas office? Your flannel suits couldn't take the heat. They'd melt right off."

"Macau then."

"Macau, Christ. Macau's worse. Face it, Frank, we're Park Avenue to the bitter end."

He smiled. Acknowledging it. Knowing himself. "Not in summer, I'm not."

"No, in summer, you're wonderful. Drunk, barefoot, and wonderful. Let's play, huh?"

Once more, I checked my watch. Then the clocks on the wall, which were still wrong.

I was the dummy. She had it timed perfectly.

"I think I'll stretch my legs," I said.

For some reason, Paulson winked. What did he think I meant? It didn't matter.

Outside, there was a trace of something bitter in the air and I could see around the strange bend in the house's western wing, out in the woods, between the chauffeur's cottage and the tennis court, the fire was going. Burning strong and gathering itself for something more. Things were moving now and there was no stopping them. It felt different than going on a border run. More so than I had expected.

From the lawn at the top of the stone stairs, I flashed a signal. It skipped over the water. The signal came back, twice the same pattern. I could hear the slap of oars in and out of the water, then I saw them coming in from the darkness. There was no moon out that night. For some reason, it unnerved me. I thought about the wreckers, the ones who cussed at the light from the moon and could work only in darkness. And I thought also about the fiddler crabs that came out to wave their pincers around for the females and the gulls that dove out of the sky to snatch them up.

Tommy was smiling and keeping quiet and focused on his oar strokes, bringing the dinghy up against the dock. He steadied himself against the pillar and I helped Marianne up. She was carrying a large purse. She looked like she had been invited for the bridge. There was more smoke in the air now. It had reached the water. I didn't believe the fire would spread quickly because the air was so still. Not even a breeze off the bay. I gave Tommy a push and he got himself turned nimbly around and was headed back for the boat. Everything on time, everyone working on rails and satisfied.

"You've got my hour blocked out?" Marianne asked.

"From right now, yes, one hour. Do you need more?"

She shook her head. "Much less. Good of you to ask, sweetie. An hour's fine."

"Take my hand. There's moss on the stone here. It's wet."

"I might need to make some noise. Not too much. That's all right with you?"

"They'll be out of the house."

"Good. You lead me to it then."

I left her in a dark corner, behind the outdoor shower, where the ground was damp.

"She'll let you in," I said. "Five minutes or sooner. Hold tight until you see her."

Moving back around the house, I saw the screens were packed with moths.

I had never called out a fire before. I had felt the urge to yell it, as everyone does, but never had an opportunity or the chance to indulge it, and it took some strength, getting the words past my lips. For a moment, it appeared nobody had heard me. The game was carrying on. I tried it again and added some detail this time about where I believed it was coming from. The smell was in the house now, but it had come in so slowly that maybe they hadn't noticed.

One more time to make it stick. "There's a fire outside," I said. "In the woods."

"Jesus," Paulson said. "Here?"

Yes, his woods, I told him. Somewhere behind the tennis court, near the garage.

"Big?"

"Getting there."

"It's probably teenagers," he said. "Sneaking in for a party. We'll go scare them."

So that was what he thought. Teenagers. Barbarians at the gate. On his property with their liquor and their bad intentions. Probably he had chased them off another summer.

He led the way out the back slider and across the lawn and into the woods. He must have known by then that it was worse than some trespassing kids. It was a full-fledged fire threatening to swallow up a small but attractive portion of his land. He stiffened and slowed. His footing suddenly unsure, walking through the thin brush past the edge of the lawn. There were other outbuildings scattered across the woods. Obscure old structures, built for different times. And clearings too. Maybe where there had been other tennis courts in the past. And one path out to the road. Packed dirt, and dramatically uneven. The town had wanted to take it over and pave it properly. The families had stopped them, even when told of the hazards. Emergency vehicles, if ever needed, would have a difficult time of it. They might never get in. That had all happened years ago and Paulson had likely been proud of it and had felt it was a victory for the old ways. The old seclusion and privacy and people looking out for themselves. He started running toward the flames now, then stopped and turned back.

"We need water," he shouted. There was panic in his voice.

I was with him. Maloney too. Elena, back at the house. He had insisted that she stay.

It seemed like madness, all those sturdy old houses, all that wealth and hardheaded economy and thrift and Puritan longing, and the roads in such poor condition that nobody even thought of calling the fire department. There was no point. We were on our own. There was a sickness in that rocky land, buried deep like a mineral deposit but permeating everything. The food they ate, the decisions they made, their judgment.

"Jesus," Paulson said. "It's going to spread."

Two, three minutes of dithering. Staring at the fire, sweating in that stale, smoky air.

Paulson said, finally, that he had a hose. He meant a garden hose. Only now remembering it. Maloney got it hooked up and we rolled it together through the brush and around the tennis court. There must have been a tap in the garage, too, but I didn't see the point of mentioning it. We got just close enough to reach the blaze and Paulson held up his arm, hollered out, and swung his arm down like a captain on a whaling ship. He had ancestors in that profession, and their portraits were hanging inside the house. Inside the den, Marianne would now be at work, Elena admiring her.

"Hit it, boys," Paulson shouted again. "Hit it now."

A sad piddling trickle came out. We worked at the knots, and it came a little stronger.

They were on well water out there. The pressure was nothing. It would take hours to put the fire out, even if we had been right on top of it. Smothering was really the only option, but it was going to cost him time to realize it. Preening around, shouting at us like we were a couple of South Pacific harpooners who would one day murder him in his sleep.

I looked at my watch. No more antiques or grandfather clocks. Fifteen minutes gone by.

That's when the rain started. You taste it first on your tongue, then it's a smell. It's always like that on the coast. Probably the plains too. Maybe that's how rain comes everywhere. Thunder rumbled through the rocky soil and shook the pines and the air wasn't still any longer. That's what it had been about all along. I had thought it was something different, something calm, but it was a storm coming in, all that evening, over the water, and I hadn't noticed. The rain started, not slowly—not at all. It was a deluge.

I've turned the events of that night over in my mind. I started turning them over then, as it was going. A good, simple plan, except we hadn't noticed the storm coming in. There was nothing in the forecast, but that's often the case. We should have planned for it.

Paulson shouted and squatted down and picked up two fistfuls of wet soil and threw them in the air and whooped. It was more a cry. He was celebrating, as though he had summoned the rain himself. Like it was something he was owed and had demanded, exercising his rights, by contract or by something else much stronger.

"That'll do it quick," he said. His voice was hoarse. His arms extended now, exalting.

A shit piece of luck. Nothing to it but luck, and it made you mad seeing him celebrate like that not knowing what it was. Not knowing anything that was going on around him. Some people get to wander through the world like that, and they live for centuries.

I thought he might go over to inspect the smolder. To confirm his suspicions about the local teenagers. Look for beer cans or footprints or condom wrappers. But he waved again, shouted something in that full-throated captain's voice, and bolted for the house.

I followed him. Nothing more for it now. No more fires to start. No stalling in the rain.

I saw a figure on the lawn, cutting through the dark. A purse over her head, getting wet.

Seventeen minutes, we'd given her. It couldn't have been enough.

Paulson was already inside and Maloney, too, shaking off his wet sweater like a dog.

I went over to the crest of the hill, where it dropped down to the dock and the bay.

Tommy was down there with the boat. He must have known, with rain, to come early.

It wasn't wrong, bringing him in on the job. He knew what to do when things broke down. Neither of them saw me. I watched him rowing back out into the darkness, leaving a streak behind, a disruption in the surface that the rain somehow preserved.

I went inside. Elena was sitting at the card table. Looking calm, making no signals.

"So much drama," she said. "All to get out of a bad contract."

Paulson liked that. He checked the scorecard he'd been keeping. Reassured himself.

All was well. The teenagers, banished. The fire, out. A nice storm rolling off the water.

We played the rest of the round, the three men stripped down while our clothes ran through the dryer, and we wore old shirts Paulson brought out for us. All of them marked HARVARD. He thought that was a nice touch. After the game, Elena told me that she and Marianne had been five minutes from getting into the safe when the rain came.

We were driving home and the night had cleared. The moon was a quarter crescent.

"She got to the boat," I said. "I watched them rowing out."

She nodded. "That's good. I was worried she might be stranded out there."

"Tommy came in and got her."

"That's good."

"So what do we do now?"

She was silent for what seemed a very long time. Her arm hung over the windowsill.

"I don't know," she said. "Nothing for a while. We started a goddamn fire."

"It was a good-looking fire."

"You would say that. Nothing to show for it though."

"Not yet."

"Christ, Jack. I don't know what to say."

"There's nothing to say."

"I know it. I just keep thinking: it would have been beautiful except for the rain."

21

Work was busy that week. I tried pushing other things out of mind to focus on it the way I had once been able to. There were a lot of house calls. It put clients on edge, having so many new people in town, civilians mostly, and not being able to distinguish one face from another. I cleaned out the drops every morning and spent the rest of the day calling on whoever needed it, bringing by sandwiches, listening to their worries. Besides the heat, it was the end of the season. Clients always wanted to leave when summer was done, whether it was a good time or not. They wanted to go home or to start something new. No more waiting around, hiding out. That's something programmed into us from too far back to change: that idle worrying at the end of a season. You could only listen to them talk and remind them of professional protocol. Sometimes you would tell them about September and how the light changed in the fall.

I was waiting for a phone call and thinking every night that she might drop in and tell me what was next. I went by her place too. There were cars in the driveway and more of them on the lawn. Six altogether, four with New York plates and another two from Connecticut. I went around testing the doors. All of them were unlocked. No alarms. Nothing valuable lying around. It was just something to notice.

I walked to Marianne's and took my drink outside. I watched the work crew putting up the festival tents on the bluffs. They always managed to finish the work in a day or so. A crew of twenty, working hard from early that morning until just before midnight.

ON FRIDAY AT SIX in the evening, a small crowd gathered outside Our Lady of the Snow, a stone church two hundred yards uphill from the harbor, on Boysenberry Street. There were a dozen men standing near a platform. They were talking anxiously, and some of them wore elastic back braces. They were going to lift the platform, which was rigged with handlebars and made of plastic, heavy wood, and some stone. There were floral arrangements surrounding the base of a long pole, on top of which stood a ceramic saint. The saint was Martha, approximately life-size, wearing a tattered blue robe. A sea bell was rung, and the men went about grunting and sweating and digging their feet and eventually they lifted her up to shoulder height. Altogether the platform weighed fourteen hundred pounds or more. They had to hold her steady for a minute or it wouldn't count. In forty-two years, the saint had never been dropped, but it always seemed like she might be. It was difficult work for the men, with the heat and the crowd watching and their mothers and the priests standing by looking anxious. Our Lady was a Cape Verdean church, but the priests were strictly Irish and the worrying types. Not many people attended the opening ceremony anymore, but I always liked to.

Father Sheehan gave a sermon after it was over and Martha was back on level ground: That Martha, the sister of Lazarus, was there to bear witness and provide hospitality, so that we might concern ourselves with others, even in the days ahead, during the revelry. When the sermon was done, the bell was rung again. It was an old bell but rang clearly.

"Go with God," the priest said, then he repeated it in Latin and again in Creole.

There were cheers from the beach. They could hear the bell and knew what it was for.

This was the start of the festival. A pure moment, and then it would go on for three nights and two days, through the weekend. On Sunday, they would grease the same pole with pork lard and hang it over the end of the pier, and some of the same men who lifted Martha would see how far they could run on it without falling into the water.

I saw Tommy there at the saint's ceremony. He was eating fried dough off a paper plate and appeared to be very concerned about the men doing the lifting, like he wanted to jump in to help them but couldn't bring himself to do it. As far as I knew, he had never participated in the ceremony. After it was done, we walked together to the tents.

"That was beautiful," he said. "Really fucking beautiful, you know?"

I told him I did, and we didn't talk any more about it. We were part of a procession of forty or so people, mostly older women in black and children drinking fountain sodas.

"Are you gonna need any more transport?" he asked. "Next week or so, I'm clear."

"I don't think so."

"No?"

"No, I think we're good. Thanks though. You did a great job."

"So, you're gonna be back at pickup this week? Should be a nice run."

"It's getting a little cooler at night."

"Right, but not too cool. We got another month outside, at least. Don't you think?"

I lost him at the gates. There were four different tents. Four thousand attended on the opening night, and some years it was a great deal more, if the weather was good. The festival meant a lot to the town. It was tradition, and besides, it brought in money.

An old woman snapped a bracelet around my wrist. Entry was ten dollars.

"That gets you two Pepsis or a beer," she said, winking her lazy left eye.

I wandered inside the main tent for a while without stopping, saying hello to people with only a wave, signaling I had to be somewhere or that I was headed to the bar or a bathroom, then carrying on in chaotic, weaving circles among the bodies and the frying stations. There were buffet tables and bars set up along three sides of the perimeter. At the center were tables, some reserved for church groups or social clubs, others open. Overhead, you could see where the fry stations had been other years by the stains. The scallops left the darkest ones. They used the same canvas summer after summer. It looked like a fresco painted on the ceiling of an old ruined chapel.

There was a lot of staff working the tent. Kids hustling clam platters and beer pitchers around to the tables. Selling raffle tickets and rum shots. Some of them carried instruments, and they would stop by a table to serenade you for a tip. The busboys worked like wildfire, sweeping away all the paper plates and plastic cups before the fans could knock them onto the ground. You would have thought the ground there would be a field of garbage, but the busboys wouldn't have it. They carried trays twice the size of what you saw in restaurants and passed them to runners, who were filling dumpsters on the western edge of the bluffs, behind the carnival rides and ticket games.

There was choreography, an art, to all that movement.

I went to look for Elena. She wasn't in the main tent, not that I could see. I found my father instead. He loved the festival. He hardly ever went out at night anymore because of the tremors, but nothing could have kept him from the tents. He was seated with a group of men I didn't recognize at one of the reserved tables. There were ten of them packed together at the small table. They were drinking and singing "E Depois do Adeus."

A few of them waved at me to sit down, but there were no chairs.

"You know this one," my father said. One of his friends found me something to sit on.

My father pointed at him, the man who'd helped me. "He was there," he said. "Lisbon."

"E depois do amor. E depois de nos." They were on the chorus again.

There were two songs that were played on the radio in Portugal in 1974, and when they were broadcast, that was the code among the liberal military officers to begin the coup, the one that led to the fall of the Estado Novo. One was by Zeca Afonso, a popular folk singer and a comrade in arms. The other was "E Depois do Adeus," performed by Paulo de Carvalho in the Eurovision Song Contest that year, a dripping, saccharine ballad that made you want to beat your chest and find a woman to leave you. That was the song they were singing: Quis saber quem sou, o que faço aqui. Quem me aboundou. I wanted to know who I was, what I am doing here. Who had abandoned me.

Ten feet away you couldn't hear them at all, they were just a table of old men with their mouths hanging open, but when you got in close the sound was overwhelming. They were enjoying themselves. My father was stoned and wanted me to stay and sing.

Every time I got up to leave, he started another verse, and the others would join in.

"My boy's a fucking worker," he shouted between breaths to the man from Lisbon.

The man balled his fists and pounded the table. He was drunk and happy.

"A fucking worker," my father said again. "A goddamn miner, out of the womb."

It was nearly 10:00 p.m. when I finally saw her.

"I've been looking for you," she said. "Christ, there are so many tents."

"Four."

"Were there always so many?"

"It's larger than it used to be."

"Something's up. I've been trying to find you. Don't you pick up your phone?"

"I've been here all night. What is it?"

"He's asking about you. I don't know why. Maybe just curious. He wanted to know about your practice. Asked if I had ever seen you in action, in court. That sort of thing."

"Who, Paulson?"

"He's got something in mind for you, I can tell. He starts pursing his lips when he thinks he's onto something interesting. Like he's posing for a goddamn photograph."

"What is it?"

"He doesn't say. But, listen, Jack—it might be something."

"All right."

"Another way in. Something new, anyhow. Christ, it's loud in here."

"It's just the first night. It's always like this for a while. It'll slow down eventually."

"You shouldn't think like that. That's always been your problem."

She put her hands around my neck. She seemed quite young suddenly.

"I saw your father earlier," she said. "He looked wonderful."

"He's in his element."

"Did he bring you here when you were younger? I always wonder about the kids."

Somebody nearby blew a whistle. Nothing happened at first, then a table of people stood up and grabbed one another's hands and they were dancing around us. Not a circle but something more serpentine, and a man in a silk vest took Elena's hand and wound her to one end, and I was ushered to the other, and the whistle blew again sharply, and more people joined the snake, which was moving quickly between tables.

The elderly woman who had taken my hand said something in Creole. I asked her to repeat it and she did. It sounded like a proverb, something about a snake, a very loose translation. The woman was wearing oversize sunglasses with pearls along the frame. She was holding on to my hip with her free hand.

In English, the woman said, "You're a good-looking boy. But not good enough."

At the front of the snake, near where Elena was, somebody was carrying a bucket of wine. A vinho verde, probably, although there was no telling, it was so cold, almost frozen. The bucket had a curved mouth, and you were meant to drink the wine that way and to pass it backward. Then the tail of the snake would somehow curl toward the head and the whole thing would begin again. The violinist was watching and seemed to control the movement of the line. The busboys were working around us.

It went on like that for six or seven minutes it seemed.

Afterward the old woman with the pearl frames said that she came all the way from Paris for this. She worked in Paris and had her children and grandchildren there but never forgot what Onset was, and what it was for. She said it like I understood exactly what she meant. She had sized me up with those paws of hers. Ran them up my shanks.

The tents encouraged that kind of talk. People forgot themselves, or remembered who they had been in another time or somebody that they had wanted to become.

I had lost Elena again and couldn't find her. The crowd was getting messy. Children were sleeping at the tables. There were more whistles and they all meant something different. Some were using referee whistles and others carried birdcallers. There weren't any more snake dances, but people were drinking from the buckets still.

It was getting late, going on midnight, when I felt the phone in my pocket buzzing.

I thought about letting it go to voice mail, but it was a work phone. There were only so many people who had the number, so you had to believe that when they called, you were needed. That was the illusion the whole thing was built on and even tiny doubts could topple it. Of all the phones I carried, I couldn't remember why I'd chosen that one.

"Is this Jack Betancourt?"

It was a distant voice. Slurred with gin. He pronounced my name in the French manner.

I always hated hearing it pronounced that way. It implied something ugly, I thought.

"This is Frank Paulson," the voice said. "Can you speak? I can barely hear your end."

He repeated the name. He was unsure of himself, or working up his nerve with gin.

I went outside the tent and found a quiet spot away from the urinals and the smokers.

"That's better," he said. "I'd like to talk with you about some work." He paused. Searching for the words, or pretending to. "I've looked into your, uh, practice. Traffic violations and little old lady wills, you said. That's okay. A man's entitled to characterize his expertise however he likes. I wouldn't hold it against you."

He was waiting for me to offer something more. I wasn't going to. Another part of me wanted to hang up, tear out the SIM card, throw the pieces into the harbor, and let the salt water take care of it all for me. But I didn't do that either. I didn't say anything.

He stammered on a while longer, gaining and losing his footing, mentioning names. People he contacted. To vet me, apparently. He wanted me to understand his position.

"The point is," Paulson said, "I asked around about you. I hope you don't mind."

He laughed. His laugh, too, was slurred.

"I learned about your practice. Your and your father's operation. I have the gist of it. I knew I had heard about your work somewhere before. From an old client who spoke highly of you. I'd like to retain you. Legal representation, security work, logistics. I don't care what we call it. We can settle the bill between us later, if it sounds agreeable."

I kept quiet and he told me he needed to make a trip to Onset. Related to the festival. Confidential work, requiring discretion. The usual terms lawyers liked to use. He would fill me in on the rest later. "Tell me, does that sound like it fits in your bailiwick?"

A cough seized him for a minute. He finally swallowed it down.

"You're at the festival now, aren't you?" he asked. "I can hear it. I've got a good ear."

There was more coughing.

"So, you've got the time to do it?" he asked. "Your schedule, no conflicts?"

I let him hang on awhile, thinking I was checking my calendar. Clearing conflicts.

He wanted me to pick him up at seven the next morning. At his boat club, not his house.

"I'm glad you came around," he said. "It was good of Elena to bring you around. I needed somebody I could trust. You wouldn't believe the people who are out there."

22

Saturday, late. All the traffic was headed into Onset, and I made good time over the bridge. The boat club was a wind-stripped little outbuilding with a deck over the lagoon and some old men hanging around telling stories that inevitably reflected well on themselves. I found Paulson inside at the bar looking quite serious. He was holding a briefcase. It was the first thing I noticed because he had it resting on his knee and his knee was bouncing a little nervously. He asked whether I wanted to sit down but by then he had already stood. He caught the discrepancy and seemed flustered a moment.

There was gin on his breath. Nothing was on the bar in front of him, but the gin was unmistakable, and I wondered if he had drunk it at home to save the money. He was dressed more carefully than his usual chinos. White slacks. A blue blazer, well-tailored.

"Good of you to come," he said. He sounded like a host

again. Like we were meeting for dinner and drinks at his club. He held the briefcase in both hands and said we'd better be going. He asked me about the bridge traffic but didn't listen to the answer.

On the drive into Onset, he calmed down some. He calmed himself telling stories. He was that kind: one made tranquil by the sound of his own voice. A lawyer, through and through. Mostly, he wanted to talk about Harvard and about sports. He told me a story about rowing crew, or rather, not rowing. He had been the coxswain on the first boat, but when he was beat out for the position by a younger boy, that was the end of his athletic career. He talked about the incident like it still stung him, being passed over, but he had finally reconciled himself to it and the tribulations of that period had made him into the man he had become, the man now sitting behind me. I was looking at him in the rearview mirror. He sat himself in the back seat without any discussion. It didn't matter; he was paying for the privilege. He had the briefcase on the bench beside him. The leather was marbled slightly, or possibly it was just worn. An heirloom.

"I don't golf," he said.

It seemed to me a wholly unprompted remark, until I noticed we were passing a course.

"I consider the game a blight," he said. "If it were up to me, I would sue the towns and force them to reclaim all the land they'd allotted to that idiotic pastime. It takes over a man's mind, have you ever noticed that? Perfectly sensible people—next thing you know, they're being fitted for pants and gloves and talking at the dinner table about moronic things: tee times and wind changes. What I'd like to do is sue the town, force its hand, but you'd make enemies that way. Instead, do you know what I do? My own rebellion. I cut across the courses every chance I get; walk right through play."

He sounds so proud of himself. He is quite drunk, I thought. He'd been preparing himself for the festival maybe, or steeling his nerves.

But for what? He still hadn't brought me up to speed. Maybe he only needed a driver.

"So what have you got in mind?" I asked. "You want to see anything in particular?"

"See what?" he asked. "Oh, the festival, right. Yes, I do. A singer I'd like to see."

I had a schedule of performances with me. "Which tent?"

"Vera Baptiste," he said. "Do you know her?"

"I caught one of her band shell shows. A couple weeks back. She was good."

He didn't want to talk about her though, and he went quiet until we saw another golf course and he began grumbling again.

He wanted a drink. He asked me if there was somewhere we could stop. We went into Marianne's, which was just close enough to the tents to be rather empty because anyone who made it that far kept on walking another quarter mile and bought a bracelet. None of the TVs were on. Marianne wasn't working. A barback named Gus was taking orders, and there were five other men sitting in there in the cool half darkness, listening to music playing. Paulson wanted gin and tonic. He wanted it made a very specific way and described it to Gus, who made it how he always did but with his back turned. When Paulson tasted it, he sighed and decided he wanted to talk more about this Vera Baptiste.

"She's incredible," he said. "You saw her sing, you heard her. You know."

She was the woman I had seen singing about Tarrafal that night in the band shell. Apparently she performed in New York, in concert halls and clubs. He had seen her somewhere in the city. The village got good performers at the festival, especially from the Lusophone world. Paulson kept holding the gin and tonic under his nose and smiling when it tickled him, like a teenager getting his first sip of champagne. The briefcase was with him still, balanced on his knee again. I kept looking at it, wondering what it had to do with him, with me, with Vera Baptiste, with his grand night out at the festival.

"I'm helping with her career," he said.

"How's that?"

"I've made sure she's protected financially. Managers can be ruthless. Accountants, same. They'll take the gold from out your teeth. I trademarked her act. Incorporated it. She'll be able to sell anything she likes—records, T-shirts, merchandise. The taxes on sales can bankrupt a musician. But I've done what I can. I want to see her provided for."

He sounded very genuine about it. Like it meant a lot to him, doing a thing like that.

I tried deciphering his meaning. Was he in love with her? In a lawyerly fashion maybe.

Then he wanted to talk about my work. He asked about the billable hours and laughed.

"I've always respected a man's racket," he said. "The hustle it implies. The ingenuity. And from a strictly legal perspective, I've always thought there was a certain right to evasion. I knew a judge in the SDNY who would never tack on the penalty for flight."

"Is that right?"

Suddenly, he was quite animated. "And my God, he was onto something, wasn't he? What could be more natural than getting the hell out of Dodge? Goes back all the way to our frontier days. Go West, young man. We need those steam valves. It's important work you're doing, necessary and fundamental. I want you to know that I understand."

He could have gone on justifying things to me all night from the sounds of it.

"She'll be on soon," I said.

I showed him the time. It was almost nine.

"Jesus Christ," he said. "It feels good to be on this side of the canal for once."

He jumped off his stool. It was a nimble, fluid movement despite all the gin. He was a pretty small guy but carried a good amount of weight across his chest and middle, so you didn't expect him to move like that. We went back outside, and the sun was down.

I felt light-headed, though I hadn't drunk anything at Marianne's or earlier in the tents.

I wanted very badly to rob the man. It seemed like he was crying out for it to be done.

. . .

SHE WAS PERFORMING in tent three. The smallest of the four, but with a good stage and sound system. The band was still getting ready and Paulson found a seat he liked. For no particular reason, I told him it would be better if I sat behind. He agreed that was quite sensible. Maybe I was his body man. He'd asked after my business and decided I was another security guard. The back of his neck, I saw, was fresh cut and a little raw, like it had been done with a straight razor. There was a trace of powder on his skin too.

He sat up straight in his chair. I had never seen anyone with such fine posture.

Vera Baptiste was waiting in the wings, ready to go. Her hair was wrapped with silk scarves and the jumpsuit she was wearing also appeared to be silk. Paulson waved to her. She didn't notice. I wondered if he hadn't imagined the connection. If he wasn't some lovesick fool who had caught her act once in New York or somewhere else and concocted the story for himself and let the power of it take him this far, inside the tents.

The house lights went down, and she came onstage. The band was waiting for her.

"I'm honored to be here," she said, then repeated it in Creole. The band was the same one I saw her playing with that night at the band shell. Three old men in sky-blue suits.

She started in with "Petit Pays," a song made famous by Cesária Évora. It was a dangerous, even a reckless choice. The crowd, many of whom would have seen Évora perform live, might have turned against the presumptuousness of performing one of her songs. But Vera Baptiste sang it well. She made it, if not exactly her own, something different, and there were people listening who could appreciate how difficult it was. Midway through the set she did "Sodade." It was the same kind of gamble and again she pulled it off. Now the people were really listening. I wondered what Paulson's face looked like watching her, what he thought of the music, and of her, but behind him I couldn't see much and, really, I didn't think about him for too long. It would have been disrespectful to the performers to worry about one man, whoever he was, whatever he was holding in his briefcase. She never looked in our direction during the performance. It seemed willful. Not exactly a snub but close to it.

At one point, Paulson turned and whispered, "She's in a class of her own."

I agreed, she was. There was no disputing it.

"I want to help her," he said. "She doesn't need me, but I can try."

He tapped his briefcase when he said it.

She was offstage then, letting the band play an instrumental number while she sipped something from a glass. I stepped away from my seat to make a call. There was mesh netting on the sides of the tents, meant to keep out bugs and mosquitoes, though it never quite managed to do it. Elena picked up on the seventh or eighth ring.

"He's got a girlfriend," I said. "Or something. I'm not exactly sure what she is."

"You're kidding me."

"I'm not."

"Who is it? How did we miss this?"

"She's a singer. Says he's helping her career. I don't know what he wants me for."

"Stay with them."

"Where else am I going to go?"

"I mean, keep your eyes open. Keep me in the loop. I'm on call too."

"What do you mean?"

"Same as you. He didn't say what for. Just that he might need me tonight."

"Need you for what?"

"He gets like this. Plays it close."

There was a long pause. I thought for a moment she had hung up.

"What are you thinking?" she asked.

"He's carrying a briefcase. Holding it tight, practically cuffed to his wrist."

"What's in there?"

"I don't know. Maybe it's why he hired me. I keep wondering about it."

"You think he's carrying them. The diamonds."

"I'm wondering. There's something about the briefcase that's not right."

"But why would he?"

"I don't know. But why did he slip out of the house? Had me pick him up at the boat club. Why did he want me along in the first place? Why me? I'm not a real lawyer."

Another pause while she considered it.

"Christ," she said. "It's possible. So, he wants to, what, show them to his girlfriend?"

"That's the usual reason for owning diamonds."

"But he doesn't own them. And they're not that kind. These are rocks, not jewelry."

"Maybe he wants her to see that he's not just some buttoned-up lawyer."

"Then what is he?"

I didn't have an answer. Before I could find one, Vera Baptiste was walking back onstage.

"I have to go," I said.

"I'll find you. I want to see this goddamn briefcase for myself."

23

The set finished and for a while Paulson didn't move. We were the last ones still seated. The show crew was beginning to close the stage for the night. The other tents stayed open until midnight. I thought maybe he was waiting for Vera Baptiste to come over finally and acknowledge him, but it wasn't that. She had already left with the band, backstage, and hadn't returned. Eventually, he asked if I would mind walking with him. He wanted to get his sea legs under him, he said. We went down to the marina, which was quite busy with people who had come in on boats for the festival and teenagers skulking about, looking for somewhere to smoke or fool around.

We walked side by side, and it seemed to me he was engaged in some kind of intense internal debate. He wasn't drinking any longer. I thought about sending Elena a message. I didn't, but she found us soon after, when we came back from the marina and had wandered into tent one. There was no live music there, only the food and the drinks.

Her eyes, immediately, were on the briefcase and then shifted to the two of us, trying to make sense of this unusual pairing and what it meant, the same as I had spent some portion of the evening trying to figure it, without any particular success, but feeling that it was somehow meaningful and maybe even auspicious. She had a table.

"Sit down," she said. "Join me. God knows I can't eat all these clams by myself."

She had a plate in front of her and a pitcher of water with fresh ice.

"Good," Paulson said. "Perfect. I want the both of you. I'm glad we're all here."

He sounded resolved, like the debate he'd been having on the docks was concluded.

Paulson was on his phone then, for the better part of a half hour. He kept trying to make calls, but you could tell that whoever he was calling wouldn't pick up the phone but was texting him back and it was making him a little annoyed. He wasn't going to allow himself to get annoyed. The briefcase was on his lap. He must have been hot in that tailored blazer. If he was sweating or feeling uncomfortable, he never mentioned it.

"She's at some place called La Vache," he finally said.

I told him it was a short walk. Five minutes or less.

"Who is?" Elena asked. Not sounding innocent but curious. Eating a fried clam belly.

He turned to her and said quite seriously, "I'm afraid I'm going to put you in an uncomfortable position. I don't enjoy it, believe me. But, if I'm going to do this, it has to be done right."

"You don't have to worry about me, Frank."

"I know. I never do. But I recognize the potential awkwardness. Please excuse it."

"Then let's go to La Vache." She ate another clam belly and didn't move from her chair.

Before we could leave, a fight broke out at the next table. It had been building slowly. Two seated men had been pushing each other from their chairs, then catching their balance and starting again, shouting things back and forth that you couldn't quite make out. It might have stopped there, but one of the men went all the way back, onto his ass, and another, not the one he had been tussling with but one of his friends, decided to jump on the one who fell, and that started the scrum in earnest.

"You're such a fucking moron, Davey," one of the men said. He had a cut over his eye.

Fights weren't at all unusual in and around the tents. The police never came inside and satisfied themselves only by rousting the drunks who slept on the bluffs and the beach, but there was a good deal of private security and locals hired as bouncers. Perhaps because of the sight lines, nobody seemed to notice what was going on. Paulson was separated by a few feet from the men who were in the dirt swinging and kicking wildly at each other. I watched as he processed what was happening. He clung to his briefcase. I couldn't quite shake the feeling that something odd and opportune was unfolding. I wanted to see what he would do next, how he would react, whether he would flee or call for help or let the paralysis settle in deeper and keep its grip on him.

Before the brawl had a chance to get any worse, another body appeared. Leaped into the middle of it. It was Tommy. He was in the fight faster than anyone had a right to be. It made me think of that night, earlier in the summer, when he had separated those kids at Alphonse's, and how quick and sure Tommy was of himself once he was on the ground. It was that way again. He had one man trapped between his legs, cinching him like an anaconda. Another, the one who had started it in the chairs, rocking them back and forth, was pinned under his chest. It was an incredible display of dexterity, or something else.

The security guards came finally and hustled the men away, except for Tommy. They must have known him. Maybe as head of Parks and Recreation, he was responsible in some fashion for the safety of guests in the tents, because the police weren't about to do it.

He looked at us and at Paulson, who was watching with horror.

"Sorry about that, folks," he said. "Should be fine now."

He didn't betray knowing us. I didn't know what he thought was happening.

A new group came along and took the chairs the men had been sitting in before. It was like being part of an organism that regenerated limbs after they were lost.

We left our table and Elena asked if we had noticed one of the men in the fight.

"It was a priest," she said. "He wasn't wearing a collar, but I recognized him."

She was right. I had seen him earlier, sitting with Father Sheehan, eating scallops.

Paulson checked his phone and said we better hurry. His pants were splattered with mud down near the cuffs. He left some money on the table, though we had already paid.

AT LA VACHE, you couldn't make it through the bodies without using your elbows to carve a path. In front was the bar; in back some tables and a small stage with a gold moon cutout for a backdrop. It had something to do with the nursery rhyme—the cow jumping over the moon.

"She's here," Paulson said. "She said she would be."

She was in a private room. There were four of them in the back. Not rooms exactly, but they were separated from the lounge and bar by wooden dividers, with panels that had been painted with forest scenes: trees, small animals, broken sunlight.

Because of the fight inside the tent and the crowd by the bar, it felt to me like we had struggled mightily to get to her. I suspected Paulson shared the sentiment. When he got into a seat beside her, it was with an unsuppressed air of triumph. She was alone, although I got the impression she had been with someone recently and they had left. Maybe it was a scent hanging in the air. Or the way the chairs were angled. She still wore the silk jumpsuit from her show and her stage makeup. It was garish up close, but underneath it she was quite beautiful. Even if she hadn't been, there would have been something impressive about her. She was nearing fifty, I guessed. Before, when I had seen her performing, I had taken her for a much younger woman.

"How good to make your acquaintance," she said, offering her hand.

She and Elena looked somewhat alike, as though they were related. A cousin, an aunt. The idea occurred to me and for a moment I felt, rather preposterously, that this was part of it: the two women were perhaps distantly related. And our meeting there, in a back room at La Vache after the nine o'clock set in tent three, was all part of Elena's plan, part of the scheme she had come up with to relieve her boss of his diamonds, and she hadn't trusted me with the true particulars but had let me come along and believe for a time that I was in her confidence.

A stupid idea. It stayed with me hardly a minute—yet the two really did bear a kind of resemblance or affinity. A waiter brought drinks and Paulson seemed pleased. Not embarrassed anymore or worried about the awkwardness of the situation.

That was when he took out the briefcase. It had been resting on his lap until then.

He laid it carefully on the table after brushing the spot in front of him with a napkin.

It was a lovely leather. I tried feeling some kind of gravity toward it—toward what was or might be inside—but all I felt was a vague appreciation for the material. Paulson undid the clasp slowly, like he was letting the moment extend. From the opposite side of the table, I couldn't see what was inside after it was opened. I looked over to Elena, waiting for her to react. Her face never gave anything away, not unless she wanted it to.

24

And if it had been the diamonds, what would we have done? Maybe Elena would have known how to manage. She had those quick, clever hands honed over the course of years: working hustles, dealing cards, carrying satchels to the New Bedford docks for God knows who or what purpose. Maybe she would have kicked me under the table, and I would have faked some kind of illness or attack. A shellfish allergy, for example. The kind that causes your throat to swell rapidly to grotesque proportions; someone has to stick a knife in to get you breathing again. It wouldn't have gone that far, but we could have made a good commotion with an act like that, and with everyone worrying over the allergic reaction and the flailing, she might have made the switch. I didn't know whether she had the fakes on her, but I presumed she had. In their satin bag, bouncing pleasantly off one another, waiting for their moment, the same as we were.

It didn't matter. There weren't any diamonds in the briefcase.

All that time spent wondering and readying myself; I might have simply asked him.

"I'm sorry to do this on a weekend," he said to the table. "But we're all together now."

"What is it Frank?" Elena asked. "You look so damn determined."

"I am. It's a small matter. Small, but delicate. It's important to me."

Finally we saw what he was carrying around all night: documents.

He wanted to make a gift to Vera Baptiste. A rather extravagant gift. He intended to transfer to her possession a property off Route 6, along with commercial licenses to operate it as a lounge. There was a great deal to sign. He laid the papers on the table.

As he went through the mechanisms, you could hear he was proud of the work.

I felt a bit foolish, having become so fixated on a briefcase. He needed only a local lawyer, somebody halfway dependable to file papers with the municipal offices.

And he needed Elena to countersign two of the shell vehicles and get them ready for their initial filings. It was all being done on his personal account with the firm and through holding companies. Legal but aggressive. And discreet, for obvious reasons.

"It's time for this," he said.

His hand was moving nearer to Vera's across the table, but they didn't quite touch.

He wanted her to finally get off the road. A woman of her

talent. He was careful to mention only her talent and not her age. A woman like that deserved a place of her own, so that she wouldn't always have to be on the move and living out of hotel rooms.

"But Frank, I like hotel rooms," Vera said. "I like being on the move. That's the fun."

"With your own club," he said, "you could invest yourself in it properly. Do anything."

"Except go on the road."

"If you want to play other shows, you can. But you'll be provided for."

"I have money."

"You have income. There's a difference, Vera. Trust me this once."

She turned to Elena. "They're hardheaded, aren't they?" Whispering, like she was telling her a secret. "I've got to perform tonight. Again. He doesn't know what that takes or he wouldn't be bothering me now about leases and licenses. About income."

But he wasn't giving up. He was ready to persuade her, pressure her even, if it came to that, but you got the feeling it was what she wanted, too, and perhaps it was a plan they had already discussed and agreed to in principle, but she felt that her pride or her independence or something else required a certain amount of resistance. Paulson was enjoying himself. Probably they had been seeing each other for a long period. Or maybe there had been an intense affair many years ago and they were thinking now about how to get back to that place. And he had come up with a solution: a club of her own. A place that would keep her comfortable and nearby, at least during the summer months.

One of the transfers, I noticed, was in Willa Paulson's name. Billie. She had signed off on her piece of it. I wondered what he had told her it was about. Maybe she knew already and they had an understanding. You can never really be sure what's going on between two people. All the bank statements in the world can't tell you that.

Of course, he had everything prepared. All buttoned up and ready to file.

"You only have to sign the papers," he said to Vera.

She was still protesting but less vigorously now.

"I've already made the write-offs," he said. "This is in my interest too."

There were tax implications, is what he meant. He would benefit or already had.

A man from the restaurant came over to talk with Vera. She was advising him about how she wanted things set up. You could tell from the detailed way she explained it that she was already imagining how she would have her own place arranged: The way she wanted the stage to look. The kind of atmosphere she wanted to project. The man seemed to be an old friend of hers. Paulson, I thought, had a flash of jealousy. The man had touched her softly on the arm.

When the man left again, she looked back down at the papers.

"So it'd really be mine," she said. Sounding like she believed it now. "Free and clear."

"With a few signatures," he said. "And your trust."

"But Frank, does it have to be tonight?"

"Why shouldn't it be? We're here, aren't we?"

"I have to perform."

"Dammit, Vera. You only sign the papers. What's there to wait for?" His tone had harshened, but only for a moment. You could feel he was making an effort to be calm. "It's what's best," he said, more gently. "I know that it is. I want you to trust me."

"I do trust you, Frank. I only want to sing tonight. Won't you listen to me sing?"

"I do nothing but listen."

"Don't be like that. I need time, Frank. We don't want to rush into this."

It seemed like a game they had played before, this back-and-forth. And would again.

"You're right," he said. "It doesn't have to be tonight. We can wait."

The man from the restaurant came back and told Vera they were ready. It was just past eleven.

"Frank," she said, getting up from the table. "You're too sweet."

After she was gone, he looked around at the papers, unsure what to do next, then finally began collecting them and restoring them to the briefcase. He turned to Elena.

"I'm sorry," he said. "I didn't mean to waste your time."

"You didn't, Frank."

"I'm an optimist. That's always been my cross. I am sorry though. A Saturday night."

He didn't include me in the apology. I felt he had forgotten about me altogether.

"It's all right," she said. "I was here already. I've been here all summer."

"Yes, the both of us. I only wish she would be too. Oh well, soon enough."

He was looking like he felt quite sorry for himself, but happily so, and found a waiter to order more drinks from. He asked for a gin and tonic with those same elaborate instructions he had tried giving in Marianne's earlier. It had to do with lemon wedges.

"I want to stay," he said to no one in particular. "I'd like to hear her sing again."

Elena asked if he wanted any company, but he didn't. They talked for a time in a quieter tone than before. There was a strange bond between them. A kind of professionalism maybe, or they had merely gotten used to each other over the years.

He tore a piece of paper from one of his legal pads, wrote something down there, and handed it to her along with his briefcase. "You don't mind?" he asked. "I might want to, well, spend the night here. You'd be doing me a favor. Another. If you don't mind."

"It's fine," she said. "I'll take care of it."

The show was about to start, and when the waiter came back with his gin and tonic, Paulson asked the man to remove the divider so that he could see the stage and mentioned to me in an offhand manner that I might send his office a bill on Monday.

I took that for a dismissal. Elena grasped him by the shoulder and kissed his cheek.

"Just get yourself home in one piece," she said. "Preferably by Monday at the latest."

"Oh, I will," he said. "We always manage, somehow. You're good to worry about me."

. . .

SHE WAITED UNTIL we were in the car to show me what it was he had handed her.

"He wrote it down," she said. "He fucking wrote it down."

She was holding the slip of paper that Paulson had torn from his legal pad and handed to her along with his briefcase. She looked like she didn't quite believe in its materiality.

"He wrote what down?"

"The combination," she said. "He wants me to put the papers away for him."

"In his safe?"

"That's where he keeps them."

"You're kidding."

"I'm not."

"The diamonds must not be there. He must have moved them or he wouldn't send us."

"He didn't send us. He sent me. Christ, he trusts me. That motherfucker."

She was angry. It had taken me a moment to recognize what it was.

"Do you have the fakes?" I asked. "You're carrying them on you?"

I don't know why I felt the need to ask. I knew that she did.

THERE WAS LIGHT TRAFFIC LEAVING town and nothing on the bridge. It felt like moving through a dream. Then we were on Goose Neck, with the tree canopy closing overhead and the gate just past the headlights, and through the woods, a gabled rooftop.

She punched in the code at the gate. She had everything now. Everything we needed.

Inside the house, the lights were off. No sign of either security guard. Asleep maybe.

She led the way to the study, removed from the wall the painting of the storm-heavy sea, and stood before the safe. She tried to slow her breathing. Moving precisely, she reached under her shirt and unfastened a clasp or a button of some kind. The satin bag fell into her palm. That was how she had been carrying the fakes—all night, pressed against her. She entered the combination. The door swung open. The safe seemed smaller now. She reached inside and came out with the stones, the real ones. She held a bag in each hand briefly, as though weighing or considering them, then poured the contents onto Paulson's desk and made the switch.

When she looked up, I saw something in her eyes: a profound disappointment. It occurred to me that we were experiencing a moment she had dreamed of many times in the past but that it had, in some undeniable sacrosanct fashion, come up short. All that planning had been useless. An errant, unforeseen moment of trust, of stupidity, had opened the door for her, and now that it was open she could barely stand the sight.

And yet, she had the diamonds. They were ours, after everything that had passed.

We left the house without speaking.

They were on her lap, inside the satin bag, throughout the

drive, which seemed much shorter than it had other times, though we were stuck in traffic and the village center was a mess with all the detours and barricades and people out walking and drinking and carrying on, hoping to wring more hours from the night.

We didn't talk about what had happened. It seemed the wrong thing just then.

"Tell me about New York," I said for some reason.

She laughed, like I was teasing her. An old joke between friends.

"It's just like in the movies," she said. "Evening gowns and taxicabs. I don't take cabs though. I always take the bus, all over the city. Crosstown, uptown, over bridges, I don't care. I like looking at things pass by. I like having all the windows. Feels like you could hop out the back any moment. The taxis are like prisons. Little roaming prisons, and some of them are yellow and some are black and they all take you to the same goddamn place. Don't pay too much attention to me, Jack. I'm talking like an old fool."

She was crying. Very faintly, but you couldn't mistake it.

PART III

25

A beach town in the weeks after the season ends is an ineffable thing, impossible to convey fully to anyone who hasn't experienced it. A drowsiness prevails. Late in the afternoon, when the wind picks up and the temperature begins to drop, you feel as though you're sleepwalking. In all the bars there's an immaculate melancholy, even among those that did well over the summer and those that are glad to be rid of the tourists for other reasons. Nearly everyone was glad to be rid of the tourists, but then there's no denying the void. I spent most of the week visiting clients to see how they were doing. You always lost a few. At the end of summer, they packed their bags and drove off. Or if they left notes or sent messages through the boards, they were long, rambling, self-negating missives full of excuses and bravado boiling down to one idea: it was time to get moving. As long as they were paid up, it didn't much matter, although I sometimes regretted the planning and other resources that had been wasted. This time, I was beginning to think of other things too. New places and landscapes. New scents in the air. Flowers blooming that I had never heard of or imagined. Sometimes I thought about Paris; other times Istanbul. The truth is I didn't know anything about those cities. I spent an entire evening looking up visa requirements, wondering about what I wanted to do and how much it would take to get started there. How much would be left over after I settled my father and the other people I was considering: a few clients who I believed would have a difficult time on their own.

By Tuesday after the festival, the motels on Cranberry Highway were nearly vacant, and the studios and one-bedrooms near the eastern end of Main Street were turning over. Teams of cleaning crews began pouring in, and the last big caravan of festival performers and workers pulled out on Thursday. You could see all the vans and trucks parked along the sidewalk on Main Street and people hanging on to bags, saying goodbye to friends, and trying to negotiate rides to New York or to the airport.

With all that activity, all those people coming and going (but mostly going), it was easy to ignore the feeling that I was being followed. In fact, that was what I did for several days, going on a week. I pushed the feeling to the back of my mind and went to play pickup basketball for the first time in over a month. My legs didn't move as quickly as I wanted them to, which meant that I was thrashed around a little and bodied up by larger men and punished for my every false start and delayed reaction. It was exactly the kind of oblivion I was after, but then on the drive home the feeling came back to me and

I thought I saw a Toyota RAV4 three or four times, holding way back, very discreet but notable for its discretion, and for its color, which I had once heard described as Barcelona Red. I went into a few soft evasions, making useless turns and parking in driveways but then exiting through the alleyways and coming out the other side.

The RAV4 was gone, but the feeling stayed with me for a time. That night I went for a swim, even though I was sore from the punishment I had absorbed at the playground.

The next morning, I went to Goose Neck. I thought I could ask a few questions about permits or filings, but Paulson wasn't there. After five or ten minutes at the gate, an older woman came down and opened it for me and let me inside. She was a housekeeper or groundskeeper. She told me Mr. and Mrs. Paulson had gone back to New York.

I asked whether she knew when the guards had left. She didn't seem to understand what I was talking about. The house was quite clean. It had a new sheen, and the floors had been polished. It seemed like a lot of work only to board the place up in a few weeks, but then I didn't know what it took to keep an old structure like that together.

I looked inside the den before going. The painting was back on the wall. The safe door, presumably, was closed and locked. The old woman asked who I was again. I told her only a colleague. I would get Mr. Paulson the papers another way.

That afternoon I went to see Elena. We hadn't spoken all that week. It had seemed natural enough. A part of me was surprised to find her still around. She could have gone back to

New York, to her law practice, everything proceeding normally. I presumed, also, that whomever she was going to sell the diamonds to was in New York and that business would need to be conducted in person.

The house was in boxes. She hadn't brought all that much with her, but she had been working from that office in the kitchen and the living room for weeks and had generated a tremendous amount of paperwork. Someone would need to come for it.

We were sitting on the porch. She was in a rocking chair. I was beside her on a bench.

"Somebody's following me," I said. "Off and on, all this week. I'm halfway sure."

She rocked back and forth several times before answering. "What makes you think so?"

"My eyes. My memory. Professional experience. I'm serious, Elena."

I described the car to her. The Toyota RAV4 in Barcelona Red. It wasn't what I had gone there to tell her. I wasn't even certain of it until the words came out and then I was. It often happens like that. All during the week I had been trying to keep quiet, lie low, having more or less success with it. Visiting Paulson's house was unnecessary and unwise, but it hadn't cost me anything. Still, I should have been more careful. Even going to see her was a risk, I knew. I knew it better than almost anyone. But it's different when you're the one being followed. When the job was yours, and now you're deciding whether and how to leave.

"You're paranoid," she said. "Try to think about it rationally."

"I know the difference. There's someone on me. It started Tuesday night."

"Then it's unrelated. That's too soon."

"Too soon for what?"

"For him to know. Hell, it could be anyone. A woman from your past. Another one."

"You haven't noticed anything?"

"Nothing. I would—I'm looking out for it, Jack, believe me."

We spoke for a while about her plans, what she had heard from Paulson after that night. Nothing much. They had talked about casework, clients, and little else.

"Who's your buyer?" I asked. "I need to know more about him."

She looked at me indulgently. Or was it something else?

"I told you everything already."

"I didn't even ask."

She paused. "He's in New York. He's going to be. He's not there yet, which is why I'm in no rush, but I've reached out to him, and he'll be there with ready cash in two weeks."

"How much cash at the handover? How much in accounts?"

"He's there to transact. Then he goes to London. Jack, what are you really asking?"

I didn't know. I wanted to hear her talk, was all. Something in the way she described the buyer made me wonder whether the man was real. She had always told me she had someone lined up. You needed to, with an item like that.

Rough diamonds. Something rare and incomplete. They would need to be transported and then cut and polished. After that nobody would be able to trace them, but before, it had to be handled carefully.

I asked her to walk me through it again, and she did. It was the same story as before.

"How could anyone know what we did?" she said. "We hardly know ourselves."

"What do you mean?"

"Walking in like that. Finding them there. There was no plan."

She wasn't wrong, but then there were all sorts of flags we might have raised afterward. Signals going up. A thousand ways to trip over a wire. There always were.

We decided to get pizza because there wasn't any food left in the house. Maybe we shouldn't have been together, but it would have been just as suspicious to be apart. The parlor was quite busy and nearly everyone there was a local. When the pizzas were ready, one of the girls at the counter would shout your name. They hired only girls whose voices could take that kind of work. Big, booming voices, either high- or low-pitched.

It occurred to me when my name was called that it might be the last time I heard it shouted that way. I didn't go out for pizza often, though the place stayed open straight through winter and was one of the few near the beach that did. The brothers who ran the place had made a good, reliable business of it. They also owned a banquet hall upstairs, an ice-cream parlor down the block, and an apartment building across the street, where a lot of the performers from the festival stayed while they were in town. It was where Vera Baptiste had been staying, in fact. She was gone too. Back to New York, maybe.

It was wonderful some years, watching the town clear like that. Fast, and without anyone having to help it. Like a strait flushing out with the tide. Full of oysters, clams.

Before we were finished eating, people began clapping. It started slowly. The Red Sox game was on. I looked at the screen, but it wasn't what they were clapping for. The division was already lost; the wild card too. It was a hopeless season. The people who were clapping were doing it in unison, to a rhythm, and finally I realized what it was for.

There was a fisherman named Tabitha who disappeared every summer. Went off on his own because he didn't like the crowds. Then he came back one night early in the fall, and he would go about getting very drunk somewhere—at the pizza parlor or the bar across the street or somewhere outside if it was a nice evening. When he was drunk enough, he would dance. Always the same dance, something called the pachanga. A faintly Latin rhythm. Tabitha danced it with his knees locked and his torso held at a slouched artful angle, like a man blown back by a gust of wind. It went on for a few minutes like that. Everyone clapping. When it was done, someone bought him a pitcher.

26

On Friday afternoon, I was sitting in the Cranberry Café, a homespun diner about two miles outside the center of town, perched over a spillway that linked the Weweantic River to a long-defunct mill. They sold cranberries in just about everything: pancakes, muffins, croissants, scones. They put a splash of cranberry juice in the coffee unless you asked them not to. In high school, I had been a dishwasher there, working weekend services, breakfast and lunch, and afterward maintained a fondness for the place and for the retired Navy cooks they always hired and stashed in mobile homes in the woods out back. Every few years, the diner would burn down. The family who owned it, the d'Agostinos, always built it back again and reopened with exactly the same menu. It had to do with insurance. I didn't know what kind of insurer would cover the place after so many fires and with all the Navy cooks living on premises, working the lines.

Somehow, the family managed to keep the business going year after year.

I was eating a cranberry muffin and reading the arts section of *The Boston Globe*. Acting natural, as I had been trying to do all week, reading about a traveling dance troupe from Vietnam that was going to perform at the Wang Theater. Sitting at the counter with a slice of cranberry pie and a coffee, reading the front page of the same paper I had taken the arts section from, was a woman about my age, wearing a white blazer and with sunglasses pinning back her hair. She was the only other customer in the restaurant.

"Would you mind if I joined you?" she asked.

I was in a booth. She came over and sat on the bench across from me. She brought her section of the paper. The other sections were scattered all over the place on other tables.

"I hate stools," she said. "They're hell on your back unless you've got perfect posture." She took a moment getting herself comfortable against the high seat back. "I'm Carolina Aguilera-Bonn. You noticed me the other day."

It wasn't a question. She seemed to have a firm grip on the tone of her voice.

"I'll bet you worked here when you were a teenager," she said. "Busboy?"

"Dishwasher."

"And now you're a lawyer. Only in America."

"I'm sure it happens like that in other places too."

She shrugged. "Sure, why not? I'm from Miami originally. Miami's not really America." She paused, looking down at the paper she had brought with her. "It's an in-between place.

Liminal space. I've said that before. Nobody ever seems to understand. Do you?"

"I know the word *liminal*, if that's what you mean."

"That's all right. I only mention it because this place, this town, interests me. I've been around a couple weeks. I rented a cottage with a name. I've never lived in a house with a name before."

"What's the name?"

"The Dragonfly."

"Before that, it was Sea Gate. The guy who owns it runs the liquor store downtown."

"Joe Gomes. Right, I looked into him. He's got five daughters. Imagine that."

She radiated confidence. Or if it wasn't confidence, it was guile or maybe tact.

The sleeves of her blazer were rolled nearly to her elbows. She poured some cream into her coffee and looked as though she were going to ask me a question about it, maybe wondering why the coffee tasted faintly of cranberries, but then decided better of it. Decided to let the mystery be. She seemed like a woman who wholly enjoyed her work.

"You're an investigator," I said. "Not a cop."

Her eyes narrowed like she was looking at me through a lens.

"Well," she said, "there's a lot to get into. I'm with a corporate outfit out of New York."

"Not Miami?"

"Couldn't stand it there too long. I like to move around. Hooper and Eliot is the firm."

"They don't do a lot of street work, I take it."

"The work's pretty much the same everywhere. Just depends who you're doing it for."

"And they're a corporate outfit?"

"In a sense. Mostly for old families who've made themselves into corporations." Something about that idea made her laugh. "Look," she said, "have we crossed paths?"

"Not that I know of."

"No, you'd remember. So would I."

We sat quietly for a time. I didn't want my thoughts to get out ahead of me.

"You know," she said, "I'd heard of Onset before. Before I came, I mean. I used to hear people talking about it sometimes. Kind of a Big Rock Candy Mountain for lowlifes and runners. The sort of place you're supposed to be familiar with in my line, only I thought, some backwoods in Massachusetts, maybe I'll get out for the foliage one day."

"We don't get colors in the trees. Mostly they're just pines."

"Pine woods, bail jumpers, and fugitives. A beach town. I like it here."

"So you're on vacation?"

"No vacations for me this year. They've got me running around on a dozen cases."

"Any in particular?"

"Lately, yup. Bill's coming due. They want a report, you know how it is."

"Who's the client?"

"Oh, the client. I was thinking you might have a few guesses as to that."

"I do, yes."

"But not eager to share them? That would expose a little too much, right? Boy, you do have a lot going on here. I don't blame you for looking at me sideways. But I'm telling you, honestly, I come in peace and curiosity. I didn't realize it until I got here. It must have something to do with the salt air. Wakes you up. Better than coffee, if you need it."

She waved to the waitress, who came over and filled both our mugs.

Her name was Kaitlin. She had been there since my days as a dishwasher.

Carolina thanked her by name, then turned back to me.

"I'm working for the fiancé's family," she said. "You know him, right? Mike."

"I don't think they're engaged anymore."

"No, that's true. You ever been married?"

"No."

"Sometimes it takes, sometimes it doesn't. You're better apart or you can't bear it."

"I'll keep that in mind."

"Anyway, he didn't hire me. He's got one of those families that views love as an inherently suspicious enterprise. They're more often right than wrong, but what a miserable way to go through life. I guess, in a roundabout way, that's what keeps the family intact. That kind of distrust. And by family, I mean the money, obviously."

"What did the family hire you to do?"

"The usual. Discredit or prove her out. Maybe find some ammunition for a prenup."

"They were engaged six years."

"I know, impressive, right? Somebody must have thought it was getting serious. You probably did a rundown on the whole family when she first got together with him. Strange bunch. Lots of eccentrics. Just to prove they can afford to be, is my thinking."

"Why are you telling me this?"

She paused for a moment. "It's shoptalk," she said. "Don't you ever want to talk with someone? You've got an intricate network going up here. I've looked into it. I did a pretty good rundown on you, actually. I was thinking you're the other man. I don't mean to offend you. But the other man wasn't the half of it. So I started wondering, What's this small-town guy doing with all those tiny little bank accounts in Panama?"

"Currency exchanges."

"And shell companies. All of them surprisingly active."

"That's how currency exchanges work."

"Right, and that's a normal activity for a country lawyer in Massachusetts."

"You've looked into me. A professional. I get it."

"Well, you know when you're doing research and you get the feeling you're scratching only the surface? Plus, I remembered the name Onset. I started wondering whether I might turn up all kinds of persons of interest if I kept poking around your currency exchanges. Then I thought, Why not take a drive up there, see what it looks like? Maybe I'd just hang around collecting names and faces and see who wants them. Turn them over to the government, the bail bondsmen, the

New York brokers. Whoever's looking for them. Whoever's willing to pay. I'd put them up for auction."

She paused to let the threat sink in. You felt it rumbling through the table.

"So, people here in town," she said, "they know what you do?"

"They hear stories. I pay some of them for cottages or rooms."

"You spread the cash around. That makes sense, but I find it interesting that you don't try to keep anything too quiet. Everyone seems to know you're in something, and yet the ones I asked wouldn't say what. I was just reading it on their faces. An open secret."

"It's something my father decided on a long time ago. He didn't hide his work."

"That vaudeville streak. Spies. A little wink for the cheap seats. Plus, people like knowing you're there in case they need you. That's right, isn't it? That's the real secret."

"I don't know. They all have a reason, I guess."

"I tried offering most of them money. Nobody took me up on it."

"I'm sure they would have if you kept at it."

"Would they? I'm not so sure."

"This is New England. We're hesitant."

"Is this the part of New England where they burned witches?"

"That's up north. The witches had their summer colony down here, later on."

"Is that right?"

"The Spiritualists. Witches and wizards in bathing trunks."

She had a pen in her hand. In the margins of her newspaper, she was doodling.

It took me a moment to figure out it was a map. The Eastern Seaboard, down to Miami.

"I like the idea of colonies," she said. "We've got them in Florida. Enclaves. You ever hear of Gibsonton? It's on the Gulf. That's where the sideshow performers used to winter. Carnival people. Freaks and bearded ladies. Nice to think they had a place to relax."

"Is that how you see us?"

"Oh, nothing so dramatic. You're more like a frontier town. A place to run to. A Greyhound station. You ever been to Port Authority at three o'clock in the morning?"

"Yes."

"My favorites are the casino buses. They never stop. It's the same principle, in reverse. Offering the same service as you, I mean. A hint of possibility. That glimpse of flesh."

"I never thought about it that way."

"You need an outside perspective sometimes. You don't think it can last, do you? How long do you figure? A few years? It was smoke screen and misdirection in your dad's day. Exploding cigars, that's how they went at Castro. I've seen the reports, actually."

I glanced down at the paper again. This time she was doodling Castro. A fair likeness.

When she was done with him, she started in on a woman. It was only a moment before it took shape. With a few lines she had conjured her up. I wondered if she had trained as an artist. Maybe all private investigators took technical drawing or caricature lessons.

"So, about what happened this summer," she said. "I know what you stole."

"What do you mean?"

"From Frank Paulson."

"I don't know who that is."

"Come now, show a little professional courtesy."

"We're not in the same profession."

"But I have sympathy for yours. That should count for something. Genuine sympathy."

Sympathy. She said the word like it was a shibboleth. And it's true, you don't come across many people who can understand how your days are filled. Not even colleagues or spouses or other intimates. It takes luck to find somebody who really cares, whatever their motives, however wolfishly they're smiling at you across the table.

"Nazi gold," I said.

She shook her head. "Try again."

"You don't take Paulson for an old Nazi hand?"

"He's not that old."

"He's got a father, doesn't he? Uncles. Law partners."

"I'm not buying it. If you'd said Nazi bearer bonds I would've bit. Not gold."

We talked about financial instruments for a while. It was getting late. Our waitress had gone home, and another woman had come in her place. I recognized her, too, but she hadn't been working there when I was around. Just another face from another memory.

"Look," she said. "I know as much as I need to. I'm in touch with Paulson."

She smiled, knowing it was something she had withheld.

"I thought you were working for Mike's family."

"I closed that report. Now I decide what to do with the surplus."

I thought about it. Surplus could mean anything. In that vagueness was another threat.

"What does Paulson know?" I asked.

"That a reputable investigator, one his firm has worked with before, wants to see him. In a couple days, I'm back in New York. I go to his office, I take the elevator to the thirty-seventh floor, and I let it out a few drops at a time until he knows he's been had but not how. Just enough to scare him. At which point he either takes the hit and goes searching for someone like you, someone to help him clear out of the country before clients come looking for what they lost, or he goes after the people who took it off him."

It all sounded quite plain, ordinary almost, the way she laid it out.

"I'll get paid either way," she said.

"So you're going to give us up. Sell us."

"Her. You, I don't know. Seems to me you might be more valuable as a colleague."

"What does that mean?"

"The people I go looking for, sometimes they run. Maybe they run here."

"I doubt it."

"You don't need to check your roster? Okay, maybe they don't. You still offer a pretty valuable service, from what I can tell. I might want to refer somebody to you one day." She pushed the pie around on her plate with her fork. "Look, I wanted to give you a heads-up. A professional courtesy."

"A courtesy. All right."

She smiled. "I wanted to talk too. See what sort of person keeps a town like this going."

She leaned back from the table like she wanted a better angle to take me in from. A moment later, she excused herself and went outside to smoke. It wasn't dark yet but clouds had come in and it was starting to look the way it does before an evening rain.

27

Elena listened to the story, then asked several questions, wanting me to repeat the details two or three times. She wanted to be sure of what I remembered—what I had heard and understood to be true. At first, I thought she was trying only to re-create the scene in her mind and to reason it through. We were standing on the porch of her cottage, which was now almost entirely packed up. She had come in from the beach and showered out back and now was wearing jeans that were torn across both knees.

"So I guess you were right about being followed," she said.

"I guess so."

"I can't help it. A part of me thinks it's an interesting turn. We've got an adversary."

"Were we in the market for one?"

"Think of it as an opportunity. A professional, and okay, she's onto us, but then we'll outflank her. Outthink her. Wouldn't that be worthwhile to try? I know, it's a bit crazy."

She was serious. "An opportunity for what?"

"If she's giving us up," she said, "why does she come to you before meeting with Paulson? She wants something. She must, or she wouldn't have come. It was a negotiation. Which means we have an opening. Come on, Jack, let's try ourselves out."

"You know that's not the play here."

"What do I know? Nothing, except some hack is following us. We know her now."

"She wasn't just following us. She knows we stole."

"Well, that's part of it, sure."

"She's going to sell us out, once she knows everything."

"But she doesn't know everything. You said it yourself. She was asking. Fishing."

Her hair was wet, and she took a towel off the porch rail to dry it.

She was supposed to have left already but hadn't. She was living out of the boxes.

"Where are they now?" I asked.

"The diamonds? Come on, Jack. They're safe. What do you take me for?"

"Get them to your forger, Benjamin. He fences too. He could move them."

"Benjamin? You're crazy. He can't move something like that."

"Take a discount. Get rid of them. Get moving."

"Get moving?"

"We've got two days. Maybe three. Then, she meets with Paulson. Then, I don't know."

"Christ, Jack. That's all the time in the world. We need only to want it."

I tried telling her again about the conversation, about what had been said and what I had heard and the way the sleeves of her blazer were rolled. How she'd made those thinly veiled threats that I believed she would deliver on. It was all coming out wrong.

"Of course she'll deliver on them," Elena said. "She'll try. It wouldn't be interesting if she didn't. I wish I had been there. Why didn't she come see me? Why go to you only?"

"A professional courtesy is what she called it."

"She said that? I knew you were leaving things out."

"She's worked with your firm before. They trust her. Paulson will let her in the door."

"And what, she'll get a finder's fee for the information?"

"She'll hook him first, show it's reliable, then take a price."

I was trying to convey it to her as clearly as I could: it was time to run.

I knew it as well as I knew anything. There was no mistaking it once you felt it.

"We get her a better price," she said. "I'm telling you, she's negotiating. She's going to get Paulson on the hook, figure the diamonds, then find out what he'll pay for what, me? For you? To cover his ass? Do you know who would pay her more? A hell of a lot."

Her eyes were brighter now. The sun was going down and she was facing toward it.

"His clients," she said. "His Bariloche Argentines." She let the idea settle. "I've got a dossier on him. All the little angles he plays against his clients. His skims."

"Paulson?"

"We offer her a piece. She can dangle it in front of them, instead of going to Paulson."

"And the diamonds?"

"That's part of it. He's crooked. They just need to be told how he swindled them."

"Told by whom?"

"Your investigator. If she knows how to barter, let her barter with the Argentines."

It was taking me a moment to understand what she was proposing.

"They'd kill him," I said.

The statement, the reality of the situation, hung between us.

"Hell," she said. "I don't know, Jack. I'm just talking. Tell me how it went again."

It was the third or fourth time she wanted to hear it. My version of events.

Out front, gulls were overhead. Carrying either clams or crabs, waiting to drop them.

"Let's get out of here," she said. "Those birds get on my nerves."

"Where should we go?"

"A ride. I'll do the driving, okay?"

"All right."

"We'll go along the waterfront. You always like that kind of thing."

I gave her the keys and we started along Shore Drive. The gulls scattered as we went.

It was odd sitting in the passenger seat. It's always odd sitting there in your own car. You can't help but see things differently. Beside me, hands on the wheel, she seemed a more physical presence. Maybe it had to do with her driving. She was an excellent driver. Not just smooth with the clutch but attuned to the landscape and this machine that was climbing through it, pawing at the blacktop and giving itself over to the turns.

Had she really learned so late in life? It didn't matter. It was a clever story to tell me and had always made me smile, even when I was doubting it and everything else about her.

She stopped the Jeep and executed an efficient three-point turn. There were hardly any other cars on the road. At that hour in the off-season it was quiet. She took us back through the village center, past the green and past the pizzeria, which was one of the few lit fronts on Main Street, then found an access road that skirted the marshes and connected, another mile inland, to a string of cranberry bogs that ran out to the town line. You could smell the berries ripening. Pretty soon they would be flooded for the harvest. The pickers would come into town. They stayed in barracks deep in the woods.

Elena had worked for the cranberry company when she was a teenager. She told me it had outfitted her and seven others in hazmat suits and sent them around the bogs in the height of summer to spray down the fields with insecticide. The heat was incredible, and it felt like you were moving across an alien landscape. After the job was done by hand, helicopters were sent to coat the berries in another chemical. The workers in the hazmat suits would get doused too. She didn't mind the work. The best part, she said, was hosing down afterward. How cold the water felt after spending all day in that suit. Your eyes would roll back in your head and you would feel your ligaments tightening.

We kept going. The bogs went for miles. People needed berries for juice, jellies, muffins, scones, cocktail mixers, Thanksgiving dinner. It was still a decent industry for the town.

She was driving too fast, as though we were in a rush. I thought about saying something to her but didn't. She knew the roads here. Later in the season, the deer would be drunk on fermented berries, stumbling into traffic unaware and unprotected during all hours of the night. But it was early enough still and the pickers hadn't arrived yet, so it felt like we had the woods to ourselves. Then the tree line sloped down for a mile and eventually cleared to reveal a small beach about a hundred yards wide. There was no parking lot. The road simply ended there.

She drove into the sand and turned off the engine and the lights. Fog was rolling in.

She put her hand on my thigh and didn't move it, just kept it there, gripping the fabric over my skin. There was nothing much in the grip, and I sat quietly and half mad because of the movement of the drive and the strangeness of being in the passenger seat.

"Let's get out of here," she said, releasing me. Turning the engine back on.

She couldn't be still. She could do a hundred other things, but not that.

On the drive back in, she started telling me again about the buyer in New York. The man who was coming to take the diamonds off her hands once they had finished haggling over the price. She had to hold out only a little longer, get her price from him, and then we could run. The way she was talking, it was hard to make out any of the particulars. Her voice was halting. Almost like she wasn't sure of the language she was speaking, which made me think back to that first summer when we were driving around marshlands and cranberry bogs and she was telling me about the school she was going to open. A school for lonely diplomats and all their fat government contracts.

About a block from the pizzeria, where the road started its climb up the bluffs, she stopped the Jeep again. She didn't pull over to the shoulder but looked in the rearview mirror and saw there was nobody around, then put it into park and stepped on the emergency break, which was a pedal in the old Jeeps to the left of the clutch. Standing on the seat, looking backward over the roll bar, she drew up her hair. When she had it fixed the way she wanted, she undid her jeans and pulled them down over her feet. Kicked them into the back seat. I took mine off. It felt like we hadn't spoken all night or had exchanged only those few empty words about driving to the beach and then leaving it again. Her legs were cold when they pressed down on top of mine. It didn't make any sense, her legs being cold like that. I didn't try making sense of it. I was just getting by, wondering what would happen next, not questioning the reasons or premeditations because there weren't any. That was a spell you tried to cast on yourself.

Down the street, I saw the RAV4, Barcelona Red, parked with its lights off.

Elena felt me tense up. "Who is it?" she asked.

"Nobody," I said. It was true. There was nobody in the RAV4 that I could see.

"Is it her?"

"No, but it's her car."

She turned around to look. I got the feeling she had seen it before.

We stayed parked there in the road for maybe ten minutes without another car passing us in either direction. It was like the whole town had cleared out with the fog or gone to sleep. She said we'd better get going. She didn't feel like driving anymore.

Outside her cottage, which was dark and quiet, she let the engine idle.

"You're scared," she said.

"Yes. Always."

She fiddled with the clutch and the gearshift, putting the car in and out of neutral.

"All right," she said. "Tell me what you want. That's all I ever needed to hear."

28

We set the meet for Sunday. No phones, an open place, a crowd. A lot of precautions whose ultimate uselessness was well known to all parties. If someone wants to listen or take photographs, they'll find a way to do it. The trick is not making them want to in the first place. There was a promontory at the top of the bluffs. A small plaza paved with flagstones. On a clear day, you could see the spires of the old railroad bridge that spanned the canal. It wasn't so clear as that but well enough to enjoy the morning air. There were benches ringing the plaza. People taking in the sun. Behind them, in a field, some kids were playing a ball game. One of those wild games without rules, only violence and a brutal sort of freedom. I arrived first, an hour before the meet. Carolina Aguilera-Bonn was next, twenty minutes in advance. Shortly after, Elena came along. We were all there, so there was no point in waiting around for the time we had designated.

"So Mike's family," Elena said after introductions. "They hired you."

It sounded like she didn't quite believe it.

"Two of the aunts," Carolina said. "Mildred, and the other one, with the nickname."

"Carrot."

"Constance Winslow. Carrot. Why do they call her that? She's not a redhead."

"Who knows? They won't tell anyone. You have to be born knowing why."

"They oversee the trust."

"That's a polite word for what they do."

"They do seem to worship at it."

"Long ago, they took vows of celibacy to better dedicate themselves to its every satisfaction and preservation. Well, they can enjoy it. None of that really matters now."

We began walking. A path, paved with the same flagstones, cut a seam along the front ridge of the bluffs. It was a narrow passage. They walked abreast and I kept a step behind. The morning was warming quickly. One last beach weekend, if you wanted it.

They were talking about Mike, his family. Paulson, the firm. Half-shared memories.

There was a similarity in how they walked. Something structural, not a superficial resemblance. A movement in the hips, and that feeling of contained possibility, a smooth transition from a walk to a saunter to a dead sprint, before you had time to think. At Shell Point, they kept walking and I hung back. It was what we had agreed to.

I owed her that much. Or maybe I didn't owe her anything but had let myself believe I might, and that was as good as the same. They found a bench but stood beside it only for a time and opted to keep moving toward the tip of the point, which would flood at high tide. Carolina Aguilera-Bonn was carrying a coffee cup. It was from Dunkin' Donuts but larger than any cup I had ever seen from there. Elena wasn't holding anything. Her hands were free. The point was empty except for a line fisherman casting from the shore and a man in gaiters in the flats looking for clams. There weren't clams in the mud around Shell Point, not for twenty years, but maybe the man knew better.

It was a long conversation. A great deal to discuss, or they were just feeling each other out. Deciding whether and to what extent to trust the other's word. Enjoying the conflicts and contradictions and everything that wasn't said in between what was.

Toward the end, Elena handed her something. I was too far away to see exactly what.

The money, with luck. Money always helps.

The plan was to buy time. Negotiate a rate, an extension. Two, three weeks. However many she could get. We would be on the move by the time Carolina went to Paulson. A decent deal for the investigator too. Nobody would know, and she would get a bonus. After her finder's fee, she could then rack up a nice bill chasing after, if she liked. Paulson would hire her for it. That was good, reliable work for several months or more.

It was better than a confrontation. Better than trying our wits out in a fight.

You never confront someone by accident. You don't confront them at all, not head-on. That's what I wanted to tell her. There was always somewhere else you could run, and there was as much dignity and peace and possession in running as in anything else. That was why you filled up the tank with gas. It was why you carried papers with you.

When the women finished talking, she came to where I was waiting. Carolina and her inordinate coffee were gone, walked off in the other direction, leaving us to sort it between ourselves. There was a seagull nearby. It kept inching closer, deciding how far it dared.

She looked crestfallen. I couldn't remember ever seeing her quite like that.

"Well," she said. "You got your way. More time."

"Two weeks?"

"Ten days."

"You trust her?"

"Not even a little. We'll have a few days for certain. Five or six, if we're lucky."

"That's good, Elena. That's something."

She looked out at the harbor, took it all in with a glance, and sighed.

"It's a tiny little thing when you're down here," she said.

"It'll look bigger when the tide is up."

"Do you remember when we swam it?"

"To Great Neck."

"And napped all afternoon in the sand."

"Woke up covered in flea bites."

"That's right. The fleas. I forgot that part."

"The marks wouldn't go away for a month. You had a cream that made it worse."

She laughed. "Your memory's not so terrible, you know that?"

The seagull was right up on us then. Looking under our heels for something.

"How much of it do you have ready?" she asked.

"Nearly all."

"Could you finish up the rest quickly?"

"If needed."

She thought about it for a time. "All right, fuck it. Soon as we can."

"You don't want to use up the time?"

"No, I'm tired of it. It's over now. Let's get moving. To-morrow, if we can."

"Tomorrow's too soon."

"You tell me when, Jack. You tell me when and I'm ready to go."

THERE'S NO ONE WAY to build up a new identity. It's easier though if you don't know the person you're doing it for, or if you know only a few pertinent facts about them and the basics of what they've done with their lives to that point. From those, you can extrapolate more freely and think about what they should have done or would have if circumstances had been otherwise. If they had been born in another place or their parents had cared differently. Not less or more, just differently. All parents care, but people all over the world are selfish and stupid, and they'll fuck you up in novel ways.

You want to preserve a little trace of that damage. From parents, boyfriends, husbands, estranged siblings, jilted nobodies, pissed-off bosses who put a credit check on you ten years back for no good reason except you were leaving with two weeks' notice. A past is a string of resentments and grievances. Grudges that never amounted to anything but were felt for a time. I paid a kid in Iceland to handle the digital traces. It might have been a pack of kids for all I knew. Healthy wind-kissed boys in front of computers, Viking aggression moving through their blood and no lands left to pillage, but they wanted money to walk around with and this was the work they had chosen.

Your identity has its components and its accretions. All the grime built up over years.

Like any other machine, you had only to break down the parts and build it back again.

29

On Monday, I bought ten pounds of clams off the docks and a string of linguiça from the Maldonado sisters on Hope Street and walked to my father's house with a shovel and rake. The food was in netted bags. There was nothing he liked so much as a late-summer clambake. To do it well, you had to prepare in advance, then hope for the best.

The first layer of rocks took the heat in well. I gathered seaweed and let the oven build. It was a beautiful piece of land, perched up high, then falling over a ledge and down onto the beach. Not a real beach but a sandbar that had spilled out of the harbor once and taken hold with a steel grip. He had his eye on the land there for twenty years before the Farnham family sold it to him. They had always wanted to turn it into a reserve. To the east of him, for miles, there was no development, only the marshlands.

By seven, I had gone for a swim and come back and dried

off. The linguiça was charred and the clams were nearly ready, but going slower. All day, he hadn't asked what I was up to. He had only watched from the window and occasionally he would stroll over with his hands stuffed into his pockets to peek over the ledge. He wanted to see that I had assembled it right—that I wasn't going to burn down his house or the marshes.

Now he opened a Sancerre. He had it wrapped in a towel and carried it outside like it was a swaddled baby. He held two glasses by their stems in his other hand. "You went down a little deep," he said, looking at the hole. "You could have lost the oxygen."

"But I didn't."

He smiled. "What's the occasion? I'm feeling spoiled. Sit down, let me serve you."

We sat in beach chairs beside the pit and drank the first glass of the wine and let the clams finish opening. It was almost dark then, and there was the first trace of the next season in the air. It always came over the water first. You could taste it on your tongue.

"Hardly seen you at all lately," he said. "Except at the tents."

"I've been busy."

"I heard. And even busier this week. You're going to, what, move her? Is that it?"

I focused on the wine. Held it up to the low sun. Turned the glass.

"How much of it do you know already?" I asked.

"I like to keep myself informed. Curiosity piqued and satisfied, ebbs and flows."

He had that wry sideways look about him and I figured he knew just about all of it.

"There were some diamonds," I said.

He nodded. "Rough diamonds, held by a lawyer in Goose Neck."

"You know him?"

"Frank Paulson. Old Cape family. Hangs a shingle in New York."

"Any chance you tipped him off?"

"Tipped him off as to what? Be specific, so later we can be vague."

"I went to a party at his house a couple weeks ago. I was there to take pictures of his safe. Later, he recognized me on the lawn. Claimed he knew me. Recognized my face."

"And what? You don't think you were that famous? Is it occurring to you now perhaps that your basketball career wasn't so storied as all that, that you're not burned into the memory of every Ivy League booster and Cambridge glad-hander who ever winked?"

He reached over with the bottle and filled my glass.

"I thought," he said, pausing a moment, choosing his words. "I thought I could help you out. Get in front of something you couldn't see. So I back channeled. It's what fathers do. That's all we do. Quietly work against dangers unknown and unforeseen."

He wasn't in a mood to apologize or even explain himself. Not fully, not ever.

"It didn't quite work out the way you planned," I said.

"No, it didn't quite, but that's the beauty of this world,

wouldn't you say? Nothing ever goes according to plan. Here's what I thought: You'd get noticed, and it would be the end of a brief, inchoate adventure with a lovely woman and no harm, no consequences."

"He'd make me and that would be the end of it. He'd guard his jewels a little closer."

"I didn't know about his girlfriend. Men like that with girlfriends do silly things."

"Like what exactly?"

"Don't you know? You robbed him. I thought you'd know how it was done."

"I don't. There was an opportunity. We took it."

"She must not have appreciated that. Not the way she planned it, was it?"

He was talking about Elena again. It really was startling sometimes, the things he knew.

People always ask what it was like growing up with a spy for a father. It was like having another father, except this one knew things. He had you sorted out. He knew all about you, and there was something comforting and almost beautiful about that, once you gave yourself over. It was an understanding between you. An openness.

"Anyway," I said. "I'm going to move her, yes. I have to."

"Whose diamonds are they? Do you even know?"

"Far enough back, some Argentines. In between, others. That's not the issue."

"No, Paulson is. The codger. The lawyer in Goose Neck. He'll spend all that *Mayflower* money trying to make it right. A respectable criminal would get the hell out of town and not look back, but not him. He'll think he's been wronged. Think he deserves better. Which makes him dangerous. He'll slit throats quicker than any crook born to woman."

"Well, maybe. He doesn't know yet. Unless he got tipped off again."

He sighed, feigning offense. "A little back channeling is one thing. That, another."

"Okay, so you didn't tip him off. Thanks for that. We've got some time. We bought it."

"So, you've been busy. But good enough to come and see your old papa with clams. Where are you going to move her to? Did she ask you for it or did you think it all up?"

"I told her what I thought."

"That she needed to go."

"There's an investigator hanging around who has it just about pieced together."

"But allows herself to be bought. For a while. Some time."

"Elena wanted to take her on. Outflank her somehow."

"But that's ugly business."

"Yes."

"You might have had to find someone to kill her."

It was the same conclusion I had come to. No other, really.

"You don't want that," he said. "You don't want anyone getting killed."

"No, I don't."

"So Elena goes. And this time for good. Never the twain shall meet."

"More or less."

"And she'll accept it?"

"She's ready to go. Tomorrow morning."

"Ah," he said. "Tomorrow morning. But tonight, clams and sausages for strength."

I could see in his eyes that he was wondering whether I was going too. He wanted to know, wanted to know more than anything, and not asking was his gift to himself. Living in that uncertainty for a while.

"Those clams are open," he said. "Let's eat before they wilt."

While we were eating, he told me a story about a play he had gone to see in San Francisco when he was young, studying at the Naval Language Institute. Sometimes you could get a weekend pass and head into the city. The play was called *Steambath*, he thought, and took place in a bathhouse. The attendant pouring water over the coals was God in the guise of a Hispanic man, and when the others sitting around the steam found out who he was, they wanted to talk about the violence and suffering in the world, and God defended Himself by saying He had done some good things too. He had made steamers and beer.

It was a story I had heard him tell before. He told it just about every time we ate clams, but it was good listening to him remember times when he was young and running wild.

"That's a good wine," he said. He had opened another Sancerre. "Better than beer."

I agreed. We talked about the wine and then, as always, came back to discussing work.

"You've got to do it right," he said. "Drive it home: she can't come back, not ever."

"She knows that."

"She says she knows. They all go back, one way or another. But tell her, not here."

I showed him some of the papers I had brought with me in an old burn bag.

"That's good work," he said. "You learned the trade. That's something, in the end."

After he was done with the papers, he wanted to know what it was like. He had never stolen something. Not for himself. He had stolen plenty for his country and even for other countries and other people who needed something from him, but not for himself.

"It must get your heart going," he said. "I'll bet that's where you feel it."

Yes, I told him, it was. That was where you felt it and it hardly lasted a moment.

"I'm sorry I tipped him," he said. "That wasn't a very kind thing to do."

"Forget it."

"I won't forget it. It didn't stop you, and I'm glad. You'll work your way out of this yet. Still, I shouldn't have done it. You don't go against your own, even with good intentions. All anyone ever has is good intentions, and they're not worth a damn. Pretty funny though, you thinking that old bastard knew you from watching you play ball."

"He hammed it up too. Made a big show of conjuring it. A real performance."

"Lawyers. They're performers, they all want the stage lights. Not you though."

"I'm not a real lawyer."

"Exactly. Give yourself some credit. You're God's own. You're steamers and beer."

It went on like that for another hour, then we kicked sand over the fire and went in.

He had bought some recordings at the festival and wanted to play them for me.

30

The pickup time was five in the morning. There was no particular reason to be leaving so early, but it made you feel good doing it before the sun was up. It was work. That's what you told yourself, and it was like any of the hundred other tricks you were going to play in the coming days to keep your mind reasonably sharp and from wandering too far ahead. Elena was waiting outside on the curb, with an overnight bag at her feet.

For the first hour, we listened to the radio. In New England, talk radio is always about sports, and it carries with it a deep vein of resentment that's not truly about the teams or the games but about something else, something permanent. If you were just going to drive around New England in circles all day, you might enter into a kind of fugue state under its embittered influence, but somewhere south of New Haven it gives out, and soon you're free. That's where we turned inland.

Off the highway and into a blind spot west of Conley, where you could string together all the local roads to get into the old mill and farm country. In and out of small, nowhere villages. We stopped for coffee and something to eat at a doughnut shop just over the New York line, before crossing the Hudson. Even from that distance, you start to feel the city's pull. All the little towns in the valley seem to be leaning away, trying to wriggle free of it, but they never quite do. Every other person you meet up there is from the Bronx or Brooklyn, even the ones who are dressed like farmhands or meditation gurus.

"How far do we stay from the city?" Elena asked. More curious than concerned.

It was the first practical question she had asked all morning. She had been making a show of trusting me and my professional acumen and she was making a show of it still.

"A wide berth," I said. "Do you need to pick anything up at your apartment?"

She shook her head.

"Talk to anyone?"

"No."

"Good. That's for the best."

For another hundred-odd miles, we were listening to the radio again. Now it was music. She moved through the stations so quickly it almost drove you crazy listening to the noise. When she found something she wanted to hear, she was just as decisive in letting go. Our phones were turned off. To keep busy when she wasn't changing the radio, she studied road maps. I had a library of them stored under the seats. Some were twenty years out of date or older and those, the oldest, were the ones she was studying.

"Did you inherit all these?" she asked.

"Yes."

She nodded thoughtfully. "You're lucky," she said. "Your father's decent."

"You can keep one, if you like. A souvenir."

"You never know when to be serious."

After lunch, she wanted to guess where we would stop for the night. She was looking through the atlases again and letting her finger fall on towns. We were passing through Maryland. Before that, for hours, it had felt like Pennsylvania would never end, but somewhere it did and you were in Maryland and the feeling transferred over with the land. I'm not sure how it was for people living there, but for those passing through, it was pretty acute, and you had to stave off the desperation any way you could think of. Her way was guessing our destination. She named a dozen places. Small towns I'd never heard of. We kept on driving until the rich damp agricultural soil gave way to rocky and erratic terrain, where the houses were built up to the shoulders of the road. Behind the houses were the hills, steeply pitched. You wouldn't have believed trees could grow there, but they did. Big ancient forest and that feeling of foreboding below.

"You could've just murdered me at home," she said. "Saved your gas money."

"You don't like it?"

"Christ, Jack. You've got a morbid sense of humor. Bringing a girl here."

In West Virginia, there's an area emanating from the Green Bank River and into the hills of the Monongahela National Forest where cell phone service falls away and devices that emit electromagnetic waves are severely restricted to keep from interfering with federally operated astronomical observatories. The telescopes are high up in the hills, out of sight. A lot of odd types move there to escape from modern technology and from other people. There are even churches catering to the influx of digital refugees, as well as the people who have come up with more eccentric theories about what the government is doing behind the fences. The area is thickly wooded. The air breathes so clean and pure you get a vague sense of euphoria while traveling the roads up and down the hills. There are a few inns and hiking lodges. They take walk-ins because the reservation systems are unreliable. The towns and camper parks are filled with people who are on the run from one thing or another. You might think that would make it a target for industrious law enforcement but that would be overestimating law enforcement. The arrest rates were notoriously low. There were always jurisdictional questions between county and federal forces, and mostly the cops just left everyone alone and tried to avoid the lawsuits that would have inevitably followed if they had tried taking their phones, radios, or, God forbid, Taser guns into one of those communities.

We stopped at an inn run by a woman I had come to know named Angela. She was always wrapped in two or three sweaters no matter the weather or if there was a fire burning inside the inn. She wore them like armor, and in fact she was one of the people who had moved to that part of West Virginia and found herself a business to live off because she believed that telephone lines and electronic signals were burning her flesh and corroding her brain. She was a kind, lovely woman, and she warmed up to Elena quickly. People always did. They sat at the kitchen table drinking tea. After the first cup, she offered Elena a sweater. It wasn't cool, but Elena must have sensed what the gesture was really about and accepted. Angela took off one she had been wearing and handed it over. It was a threadbare cashmere sweater. Green, like the looming trees.

Later we sat by a fire. It was roasting warm inside, but the fire felt good.

Angela had gone to bed and left us alone, very discreetly, believing we were on the run.

She believed everyone was. She was a romantic.

"I like her," Elena said. "I'm glad you brought me here. I was mean about it before."

"It's a good place to hide a body."

"You haven't ever done that, have you?"

She was smiling cruelly. Or it seemed cruel to me, somehow.

"No," I said. "I've never even seen a dead body."

"That's a lie."

I shrugged. "Have you?"

It was an absurd thing to discuss just then. Like we were children.

"Can I see the documents?" she asked.

I was carrying them still in the burn bag. Old material, near to dust. The papers spread across the table and for a moment, while she was sifting through them, reading the names and dates and absorbing everything, the details of her new life, I had a feeling she was going to throw them all into the fire. Burn them down to ash. I don't know why.

Instead, she began to laugh. It was a wild laugh that startled me.

Then I remembered: it was the first time she'd seen the name. The one I'd given her.

"I'll finally get to try it out," she said. "It was good of you to remember, Jack."

I figured she deserved it. A Kennedy, at last. A distant cousin. Or by marriage. A farce.

She was looking at one of the visas. There were four of them. Different entries, exits, durations. I had been keeping busy all week working up the contingencies and details.

Every now and again, as she looked through the dossier, she would start back into laughing. At ten, we went to bed. There were no electric lights inside the house, only candles and lanterns. We had been using one of the lanterns to look at the papers. Probably that was why it had taken her so long to realize what name I had given her.

Mariana Lopes-Kennedy. It was a good name to travel under, I thought.

IN THE MORNING THE FLOORBOARDS were cool underfoot, but as soon as the sun was up over the tree line it began to warm and the dogs came down from the hills for their breakfast.

Angela fed the dogs and introduced them to us, naming

each one and waiting for us to say hello, how are you. It was all very cordial. We decided to stay for the day. How the suggestion first came up, I don't know, but it was made sometime while we were visiting with the dogs, and later Elena asked if we could take them for a walk up the hill.

"They'll take you," Angela said.

She was proud of them. They were frenzied but kept to a good, tight pack.

We walked the old hunting trails in the woods and stopped by a stream where the dogs wanted to bathe. It was a raucous scene. They jumped into the water in unison and wrestled there for a while, and one of them came over to see if we wanted to join. The dog's name was Jacob. Very solicitous and concerned, albeit a little high-strung. Elena took off her shoes and waded into the middle of the stream and sat down on a rock where the water could run over her feet. The dogs splashed around and sometimes nipped at insects hovering over the water's surface. Around noon, we went in for lunch.

"We're lotus-eaters," Elena said. It was a sudden, unprovoked observation.

Angela had left sandwiches for us. She was attending afternoon services, the note said.

She belonged to a church of people who were sensitive, like her. That's the word she used. Some of them called it an allergy and others described it as the grand awakening.

"What do you mean?" I asked.

"It's the kind of place you mean to visit and end up moving to and later on you can't explain it to anyone. Why you made the decision. It doesn't feel like a decision at all. You're just sinking into a warm bath, and they keep gorging you on all of those lotuses."

"Does that mean you like it?"

"Very much."

"How long should we stay?"

"And tempt fate? I don't know, Jack. You decide. I'm along for the ride."

We stayed another night. At around three in the morning, I woke up to a noise. Footsteps. The floorboards were old. You couldn't keep any secrets in a house like that.

Before I was fully awake, I had a thought: Elena had taken the passport and was leaving. Running with the diamonds and her new identity. She didn't need me for anything. I was vestigial. The papers were solid enough to cross any border she liked.

We were sharing a bed. She was beside me sleeping. She slept so deeply it made you want to reach a hand out and touch her back to make sure that she was still breathing.

I went downstairs to look and saw Angela in sweatpants, wearing three or four sweaters. She was standing by a glass sliding door, looking out back, toward the hills.

"Where do you think they go at night?" she asked.

I thought she meant the dogs. I looked outside and saw they were on the back porch, sleeping on a pile of blankets laid out there. I didn't know who she meant. She wasn't talking to me, as far as I could tell. I went back upstairs and got into bed, which was an extravagant custom bed, king-size at least, with elk horns carved into the corner posts.

In the morning I left money and a note. Angela wasn't awake

yet. She liked to sleep in unless somebody, a guest, wanted her to cook breakfast. Elena left her a note, too, and was careful that I not look at it. She said that it was a secret, something between women.

I HAD NEVER MADE SUCH a long drive with someone I knew, except my father. Hours passed without either of us speaking or looking at each other. Like we had disappeared. She was flipping through the atlases again, glancing at them idly, bored.

We were near the Tennessee border, keeping mostly inside North Carolina, going south.

I told her there was something I needed to know: How was she carrying the diamonds?

She was leaning back in the seat with her bare feet on the dash and the window open.

"I got rid of them," she said. "They're gone."

"What do you mean, they're gone?"

"I gave them to that investigator with the lovely name, Carolina Aguilera-Bonn."

"No you didn't."

"Why would I lie to you, Jack?"

I could think of a hundred different reasons why.

She brought her feet down and turned herself around to look at me squarely.

"You were scared, Jack. Scared for me. It was wonderful. I could feel how scared you were and I didn't want that for you, so I sold her the diamonds. I was out of pocket seven thousand on the preparation, so that's what she gave me. We're back to even."

"What are you talking about, Elena? You're carrying them with you now."

"I'm not."

"Then where are they?"

"Wherever she took them. It was never about the diamonds, Jack. You know that."

I was concentrating very hard on the road and on not looking at her. I could feel that what she was telling me was the truth, and I didn't need to look at her to confirm it. Even if I had, what good would it have done, staring at her face? I kept to the road instead. It was swollen along the flanks. There must have been a flood that had receded.

"It felt good getting rid of them, Jack. I never wanted them like that. It was so ugly."

"The money would have been nice. It wouldn't have been ugly at all."

"Yes, it would have."

"Then what are we doing, Elena? Why are we on the goddamn run?"

She let the question hang around for a time before answering.

"We didn't manage a proper heist. At least we can make a decent getaway."

She was waiting for me to laugh or smile or say all right, but I wasn't going to do it.

"We can't trust that investigator," she said. "All I did was buy us some time. A little more than I let on, but it's all the same, really. You said get rid of them. Take a haircut."

"I didn't mean like that."

"Don't be upset. You wouldn't be upset about something like money."

"Wouldn't I?"

"You were a lot of things but never squalid. You can still go to Paris. Hell, you're sending me somewhere. You can send yourself to Paris if you want. You can make a living there or anywhere else, because you've got transferable skills. You're a dancer."

Still waiting for me. Wondering when I would crack. Enjoying the challenge of it.

I realized then that she must have known I wasn't traveling with her. I thought maybe she would be wondering about it and I would have to tell her at some point that she was going alone—that everybody always has to go alone because together you'll get caught. It's inevitable and there was no point fighting it. Running was just something you had to do alone. There were plenty of things like that and running was one of them.

"Tell me how it works," she said. "Will you check in on me now and then?"

"Yes," I said. "Now and then."

"You'll be the only one in the whole world who knows where I am. That's incredible."

She sounded exhilarated at the prospect. Like it was all she'd ever wanted.

We drove in silence for twenty or thirty miles after that. The car felt lighter, quicker, now that I knew there weren't any diamonds with us. It was absurd, but that's how it felt to me, and I tried holding on to it for a while and thinking through what it meant. The diamonds were with the investigator. She could sell them back to Paulson and claim a fee or try to sell them herself and work around him, if she was willing. Elena was whole on her expenses. The job hadn't been the way she imagined it, anyway. Cresting a hill, it almost felt like we'd left the pavement.

Another twenty miles on, the feeling was gone. You could only hang on to it so long.

"Play a game with me," she said. "Tell me one place you'd like to move. Not to visit and not only to live, but a place you'd like to start a family. A legacy, you see what I mean? Somewhere you'd like to get married to a local girl and knock her up five or six times; they all survive and have children of their own and one day you're a happy old man, with all your heirs sitting around a long table, listening to your jokes and stories."

I thought about it for a while. It seemed a very serious question.

"Foreign or domestic?"

She shrugged. "It's your life. Your legacy."

"Marseille."

"Not Paris?"

"No."

"Marseille, what kind of answer is that? You're a secret Francophile."

"You asked."

"I didn't think you were going to say Marseille. Christ, Jack, you're all right. You are."

"What about you?"

She shook her head. "It's not my game. I just wanted to know about you."

We didn't talk for a time after that. Ten or fifteen minutes. Then she asked me to tell her everything I knew about Marseille. It wasn't a long conversation. After five or six things I had read in books, I began telling her things I was making up or speculating about. Marseille was an answer that had surprised me. I knew almost nothing about it.

"Tell me something else," she said. "You don't regret working with me, do you?"

"Is that what we did?"

"Don't be an idiot. I'm asking you a question. What else have we got to do?"

The radio had given out. The hills, steeper now, were blocking the signals.

"No," I said. "I don't regret it."

"I take you for granted; I know that I do. Don't think I'm too heartless though. Everybody's got to take someone for granted. We'd go fucking crazy otherwise. I just hope I didn't disappoint you. I'll make it all right. There's plenty of time for all that still."

We were coming down out of the hills by then. She sounded hopeful and convincing.

FOR ABOUT SIXTY MILES we followed the course of the Savannah River. There were little towns out there that looked like pure swamp or marshland and it made you feel like you were getting near the coast. You weren't, but it's a tricky river and there were plenty of good, meandering roads that would lead you south and east without being too direct about it. We crossed into Florida midafternoon and kept going down the center so long as there were roads. Florida wants to push you over toward one of its coasts, but if you're determined about it you can keep to the interior for a long way.

We stayed the night at a hunting lodge about a hundred miles north of the Everglades. It wasn't a place to linger. There were no lotus-eaters there, just a pack of sad drunk men discussing boar. That's what they were there to hunt. The boars were a pestilence. The state would let them kill as many as they wanted, and that's what they aimed to do.

We cleared out early and finally committed to a coast. She must have had an idea where we were headed by then. Once you're on the Atlantic, with all that momentum headed south, there are only so many options. We were back on highway. There were traffic jams starting around Port Saint Lucie and more of them in Jupiter, Boynton Beach, Delray.

In one of the traffic jams, there was a man walking in the breakdown lane with a sign overhead telling you to ask him for the truth about the Kennedys in Palm Beach. It seemed to me an extraordinary coincidence. Then again, Palm Beach had been full of Kennedys once. Winter dances and weekends away from the White House. All of them dressed in dinner clothes, dreaming up an aristocracy. Elena didn't notice the man at first. When finally she did, she rolled down her window.

"What is it?" she asked.

The man sauntered toward us, weaving through the cars,

which had begun to move again, though only a few yards at a time. He carried the sign under his arm.

"Twenty bucks," he said.

"What for?"

"The information. You want it, don't you?"

Elena gave him a five. He held it up to the sun, which was merciless at that hour.

"You with the government?" the man asked.

"He might be," she said, pointing to me. "I'm not."

The man looked at me, a little disgusted, but he didn't walk away. He leaned in close.

"You don't want to know," the man said. "That's the truth."

Elena smiled. "Sure I do."

The man shook his head. "My dad, he ran with them. I ought to know."

Traffic was starting to move again. The car in back of us honked.

"Look," the man said. "I could tell you about the women, but you'd never believe. You've got to see it for yourself. Go to this address. Go and see it with your own eyes."

He held up his hand. His open palm faced toward her and held steady so she could get a good, clean look. It was blank. Maybe something had been written there once. Not anymore. Now it was just flesh, plump and delicate. It looked to me like a priest's hand.

I put the car into gear and we inched up. The man went back to the breakdown lane. The sign was over his head again and he was walking north, against traffic, sauntering.

"I guess I had that coming," Elena said.

"You only gave him a five."

"You think I got a quarter of the truth?"

"Maybe. Or it was invisible ink. You shouldn't have told him I was government."

She shook her head. "It's all right. He got me pretty good. He deserves the five."

I got off the highway for a while and drove inland. There was only so far you could go before running into the swamps. We came into Miami from the west and picked up the river. The neighborhoods out there were clustered around shipping depots. Big sunbaked parking lots filled with moving trucks and people trying to send packages to friends and family in Caracas, Havana, Port-au-Prince, Santo Domingo. The costs were relatively low. They piled the packages into trucks and drove them to boats that were full to bursting, and on the other end were swarms of men waiting with flatbeds and motorbikes who would finish delivery by hand within a day or two of the boats' arrival. Customs didn't pay much attention. I had worked with a few of the operations there in the past but not for a long time, and it seemed likely to me that everyone I once knew there was gone.

We stopped to eat on the side of the road. There was a truck with a spit roaster in the back and they were selling whole chickens from it with potatoes that were on the bottom shelf of the roaster collecting the drippings. Beside the truck were picnic tables.

We didn't talk much, though we must have stayed there on the roadside for an hour or so. We were speculating about the Kennedys in Palm Beach. Had someone been killed, like in Chappaquiddick? Had an election been bartered? Maybe it was something smaller. A shady real estate deal. A nephew or a niece stashed away in a private clinic.

We got back on the road, both of us more pensive now and full of chicken and potatoes. It was four in the afternoon by the time we reached the water's edge. The Atlantic catches you off guard that far south. The water has that obscene tropical brilliance.

There was a traffic backup at the Rickenbacker Causeway and another man carrying a sign overhead. It looked like an election sign. The name didn't mean anything to either of us. The man holding it was extraordinarily sunburned and had a look of supreme arrogance on his face: so certain in his cause and jubilant about whatever minor scandal he and his poster were eliciting from the public that was waiting to pay a toll and drive to the key.

"They must spend a fortune on poster board down here," Elena said.

She was leaning on the windowsill again, watching it all pass by like a dream.

THE MARINA WAS BUSY. Boats coming in from fishing junkets. More sunburned men and some kids who appeared not to have eaten enough or they were pumped full of nausea medicine. Little guys in polo shirts were working the docks, collecting their tips.

It looked different in the daylight. We walked by the slip where I had brought the Stamford kid, and I remembered how the smaller man of the two I was dropping him with had disappeared into the hold and it had taken me minutes to notice he was gone.

We were seven slips down from there. I was counting boats along the way. An old habit.

Her ride was a thirty-seven-foot whaler with a covered cockpit and a tuna tower that had been added recently. A good charter boat with a captain who knew the islands.

"Is this when you tell me where I'm going?" she asked.

"Do you want to know?"

"No, I don't mind it like this. It's better this way."

I gave her the name of the woman on the docks at the other end, who would take her on the next leg and was a cousin of the captain and wouldn't need to have anything explained. Then there would be three more handoffs to people I had worked with.

"I'm just realizing," she said, "how much this cost you. I can't believe I didn't think about it before, and I was thinking only about my lousy seven thousand out of pocket."

"That's all right," I said. "It's all overhead for me."

She squeezed my arm. "You were never squalid. A lot of things, but not that."

I had thought she would have the diamonds to sell on the other end and that this would finance everything she needed and a great deal more, but it was okay not having them.

It would have to be okay. She would have to start from scratch.

A short time later, while the captain was still readying things, she asked what would happen if she ever went back to Onset. If she ever got the urge and just traveled back.

"Maybe nothing," I said. "But it would be better not to."

"You think someone would try to have me killed?"

"It's possible."

"That's because you're a sentimentalist. I've always said so. I won't come back, okay? And if I do, you'll be the first to know. I'll show up one day, knock on your door, and you'll be frightened for me, but it'll be fine. We'll go around with the Kennedy papers."

"Doing what?"

"Anything we want. There's nothing you can't do with the Kennedy name. We'll start out filching drinks and work our way up from there. All right? That's what I'm going to do wherever you're sending me. I'll start out filching drinks and then see where it takes me. It was good of you to think of the name, really, Jack. Read all the international papers. You'll read about me someday. Exiled Kennedy pulls off daring daylight theft."

"What are you going to rob?"

"Oh, whatever's lying around. I'll wait to see where I am, to find out what's good."

"Paintings, jewels, scrimshaw. Maybe some rough diamonds."

"Sure, anything. It doesn't matter, does it? I'll manage gracefully. You can read about it."

She was hanging over the rails now, looking at the bay, which at that hour, in the late afternoon, was an iridescent green, and beyond it was the city, muddled from the heat.

She sounded eager to begin. To get out on the water. To be in the next place where she would have to live by her wits and would manage it well and gracefully, as she said, and it didn't matter whether she was a Kennedy or a Lopes, she would enjoy the opportunities in front of her. Maybe that was all she had ever wanted: raw possibility.

That was what I told myself, but the eagerness may have only been a sleight of hand.

Finally, the boat was ready and the captain said it was time. I helped with the dock lines. They were tied to the cleats with a knot I'd never seen, something very simple that held tight but was quick to unfasten once you figured it out. I thought about asking the captain what the knot was called but decided it was better not knowing. I could enjoy it.

Elena was still hanging on the rails as the boat started leaving from the dock. She had told me not to wave as they left and she wouldn't wave either, but she did wave. As she did, her shirt lifted slightly and I thought I saw something dark against her flesh. It looked like the satin bag she had been carrying the diamonds in. Clinging to her, wrapped with a band, pressed against her skin. The same way I had seen her carrying them once before.

Not a bad way to transport, although at customs she would need to do better.

So that was it, she had finally robbed someone. A plan, well and truly executed. A mark, taken for a fool. Or maybe I had imagined it. From that distance, it really could have been almost anything. I stayed on the dock a few minutes more, watching them vanish.

31

It was a Thursday when I got back to Onset. The last leg of the drive home was a long one. I had spent a few days in West Virginia by candlelight and played around with the idea that I might stay, knowing I never would. Wondering about things seen and unseen. All that possibility, which she had wrapped up like a gift, instead of the money.

By the time I got into town, it was just after seven o'clock. Dusk, that time of year and getting cooler. There was more salt in the air, or it was the same salt as always but you could feel it more, without the heat, and the paint on all the cottages seemed to be wearing away under its influence. Come spring, they would have to be painted again.

I went by the cottage where she had been staying. Boards over the windows already. No signs that anyone had been there recently, except the rosebushes were still in bloom.

I drove straight to the playground. From a half mile off,

you could see the lights over the court, and a little closer you could hear the scuff of sneakers and the reverb of the ball and the gulls who were squawking overhead. There were always gulls over the courts, especially when the lights were on. They liked to use the blacktop to open up the crabs.

My legs loosened up after a game and the ball felt good in my hands. It was a leather ball that had been used indoors, on wood, for several years and was getting its first run at a second life on blacktop. The sand was only beginning to work itself in between the knobs and seams. The ball rolled right off your fingers, and with a flick of the wrist, it felt like you could alter its flight even after it had left your touch. Maybe you could. Maybe there was a physical connection between you that extended farther than the flesh, an electric charge or current that ran through the air, and with enough whip or torque, you could affect its trajectory. Probably not, but that's how it felt with good leather balls.

Later at Alphonse's, I was sitting with Tommy. He and I had played together all night. We were trying to talk about the sequences of plays that had bewitched us, but you never remember them the same. You're always talking at odds. The experience was collective but not the memory.

We had hit an impasse. It was at that point that Tommy might have busied himself with the beer, as I was doing. But he wasn't drinking much, so instead he asked about Elena. He hadn't seen her for a while, and he thought that maybe I knew where she was.

"You guys were thick for a bit," he said. "Things change, I guess."

"I just dropped her off a few days ago."

Tommy nodded like that was what he had expected to hear. It made perfect sense.

"Oh yeah," he said. "I didn't see you around this week. Where you been?"

"Miami. I left her at the Rickenbacker Marina. She was going to travel to an island."

"Oh yeah? Must be nice."

"Traveling alone. With some diamonds, or not. Maybe working with a private investigator who's been hanging around looking for an opportunity to double-cross someone. Or it's a triple cross, and Elena's ahead of it. Doesn't matter. She didn't care about diamonds. Or the money. Wasn't about that. She'd be fine starting over with nothing. She'd be happier that way. In five years, she'll be running a language school."

Tommy was still nodding along. He was a good listener, when you wanted one.

"You got to take a bet sometimes," he said. "Otherwise, what's the point, right?"

"I don't know. I miss her when she's gone."

"That's all right. Hey, you ever notice, she's always bumming rides?" He was smiling a little ruefully. A pleasant memory. "I wonder why she doesn't just buy a car."

"She didn't know how to drive until late."

"Nah, get out of here. You think so?"

"That's what she told me."

"Even still, she could have bought a car at some point. She had money, believe me."

I did believe him. Sometimes when he spoke, it all sounded so perfectly simple.

Later, the tables started to clear out. It was a pleasant night. I wasn't in any rush.

"I'm thinking about going to India," Tommy said. He was looking over toward the harbor like it was where India was. "Probably not right away but pretty soon. A month."

"For the yoga?"

"Fuck you. I could do yoga. You think all those gurus didn't start somewhere before they got paid? That's not the India I'm talking about. I'm talking about up in the mountains. Might as well be Nepal or Tibet or wherever. Just depends on which valley."

"Which valley are you going to?"

"Parvati Valley. Way the hell up there. And I'm not gonna be doing yoga either."

He paused and waited for me to ask what he was going to be doing.

"There's all these lost kids up there," he said. "They disappear every year. Dozens. Backpackers and hikers and kids who are just out wandering. I'll go and look for them."

He sounded very genuine about it. I didn't think he had ever hiked a day in his life.

"Some of them get robbed or drugged or they drug themselves, you know? They get caught up in shit so deep they can't see out. They could use a hand, but who's gonna help them? The consulates don't care. They're way the hell on the other side of the country. Plus, you need real juice to get a consular affairs officer away from his desk."

"What if the kids don't want to be found?"

He shrugged. "That's fine. They tell me and I'll relay the message. They make a lot of hash up there. That's one of the valley's big exports. Some of them, that's why they want to stay. Maybe I could get ahold of some. Bring it home for your dad to smoke."

"So either you'll be an investigator or a drug smuggler?"

"That's true," he said. "I'd be investigating, huh? That must be why I wanted to tell you. Because earlier, you were talking about your friend. That private investigator."

It all made sense when you looked at it right. I ordered another round of drinks and Alphonse brought them out himself and sat down at the table to talk. He and Tommy were second or third cousins. For a long time, they had held a steadfast grudge against each other for reasons I had never heard adequately explained. It appeared as though they'd squashed it and were back on friendly, if guarded, terms.

Alphonse thought India was a decent idea. Everybody did, especially Tommy.

He wanted to know if I could make him up some passports to take along. Blank passports, like a check that hadn't been filled out yet and could be used later on, freely.

He was thinking it would be useful to have a Canadian passport. Maybe Russian too.

I told him it didn't work like that. He seemed pretty disappointed.

Alphonse lit a new cigarette and handed it to Tommy. A kind, familial gesture. He was working the place alone. All his nephews had gone back home at the end of the season.

In the center of the table, like a floral display or a candle, was the ball we had been playing with earlier. It was one that Tommy had brought along. I asked where he got it.

"I don't know," he said. "Found it, I think."

"You didn't find that ball."

"Why not? I could find a ball like that. I find things all the time, you don't even know."

"I'll buy it off you."

"This ball?"

He held it up to catch a glint of streetlight, then turned it over like a glass of wine.

"How much do you want?" I asked.

"I'm keeping it," he said. "It's not for sale."

We started haggling. We began pretty far apart, but Alphonse was there, and in his grave, dour presence, neither of us had the temerity to take too extreme a position. Finally, we settled on twenty dollars. Tommy said that I should consider it a donation. I figured he meant a donation to the Parks Department, from which he had no doubt taken the ball.

He put the money into his pocket. "Every twenty I collect, that's another lost kid in India."

He meant it too. What could you say to a guy like that? I gave him another twenty, settled up with Alphonse, and said good night to the rest of the guys hanging around.

Walking home, I had the ball to keep me company. I didn't dribble much. It was late and the town was quiet. I didn't want to wake anyone, so I just bounced it now and again off the grass, which muffled the sound, and tossed it overhead, letting it spin off my fingers. That was why I had bought it, for that feeling. It would only last a little while longer. For a few days, if I was lucky. You could sense it wearing down all the time.

ACKNOWLEDGMENTS

Thanks to:

Jack, Kathy, and Franny Murphy, and that house full of books.

Wareham, Massachusetts, my hometown, my inspiration.

Duvall Osteen and the team at Aragi, Inc. Brooke Ehrlich and the team at CAA.

Ibrahim Ahmad, Bennett Petrone, Mary Stone, Alex Cruz-Jimenez, Johnathan Lay, and everyone at Viking who worked on this book.

My colleagues at *Lit Hub* and *CrimeReads*.

All the lawyers, judges, and colleagues who advised me on fugitive matters.

All the pickup basketball games in the world, especially the ones I ran with for a time.

Dan, Derek, Tim, Kristen, Emma, Caroline, Liz, Ian, and others who shared memories.

Leonardo, Gisela, Adriana, Ignacio.

The Wareham public schools, the Wareham Free Library, and the Spinney Memorial Branch, the Kennedy family, Marc Anthony's La Pizzeria, Leonard C. Lopes Memorial Park, Water Wizz, Cranberry Cottage, Plymouth County DA, and various beaches, playgrounds, and hideouts.

And most of all, Carolina and Eloisa, my beating heart.